HOLLY COTTAGE
A SHORT STEAMPUNK ADVENTURE

SHELLEY ADINA

Moonshell
Books

Cover art by Seedlings Online

Holly Cottage / Shelley Adina -- 1st ed.

ISBN 978-1-939087-93-5

❀ Created with Vellum

The Magnificent Devices series
Lady of Devices
Her Own Devices
Magnificent Devices
Brilliant Devices
A Lady of Resources
A Lady of Spirit
A Lady of Integrity
A Gentleman of Means
Devices Brightly Shining (Christmas novella)
Fields of Air
Fields of Iron
Fields of Gold

Carrick House (novella)
Selwyn Place (novella)
Holly Cottage (novella)
Gwynn Place (novella)

~

The Mysterious Devices series
The Bride Wore Constant White
The Dancer Wore Opera Rose
The Matchmaker Wore Mars Yellow
The Engineer Wore Venetian Red
The Judge Wore Lamp Black
The Professor Wore Prussian Blue

INTRODUCTION

Buying a cottage is not as easy as you'd think. Especially if you're a man with a past ... in love with a woman with a future.

Maggie Polgarth astonishes everyone at Carrick House when, in a bid for independence, she buys a plot of land and a cottage near Vauxhall Gardens. From one decision, change ripples outward in the flock. Maggie transfers her scientific studies from Munich to London, leaving Lizzie behind. Two of the street sparrows leave the Malverns' protection to go with her to her new home. And most significant of all, she meets a man who is not only well educated but also kind and handsome.

But the south bank gangs have not forgotten the Lady of Devices. If they cannot touch her, it's only a matter of time before they take their revenge on someone closer to hand. Jake Fletcher McTavish will risk his own life before he allows anyone to harm a hair on Maggie's head. He's not afraid of the gangs and he's a dab hand in a fight. But how can he show Maggie that his feelings run deeper than those of a brother? And how can he protect her when she seems to prefer the company of her new suitor—a man who is everything Jake is not?

If you like old-fashioned adventure, brave women, clever children, and strong-willed chickens, you'll love this short story set in the Magnificent Devices steampunk world. *Fangs for the Fantasy* says, "The backbone of this great series is and has always been the characters. Their issues, their layers, their complexity, their solid relationships and their loyalties all elevate a good book to a really great one."

"It's another excellent chapter in this ongoing epic adventure of this series. I love this world and the story of these excellent women and the saga will never end. No. It will not."

— FANGS FOR THE FANTASY, ON FIELDS OF IRON

"I love how we can have several capable, intelligent, skilled women who are happy to work together without competing, without hating each other, without unnecessary dislike or conflict, without jealousy, without rivalry but with genuine friendship and respect. ... All of this comes with some excellent writing."

— FANGS FOR THE FANTASY, ON FIELDS OF AIR

HOLLY COTTAGE

London

*D*earest Maggie,

     In only two months you will be home for Christmas! This term has gone unaccountably slowly. Dr. Malvern and I have had to break ourselves of the habit of standing in puzzled reverie before the brass cylinders of the calendar, unable to account for the plodding pace of the cogs until you and Lizzie are with us again.

     That said, we are busy as usual. After our presentation of the Apollo Veil to the Royal Society of Engineers, and the simultaneous publication of a monograph authored by us both, we have had two major investors come forward—one of whom is your own Uncle Ferdinand, Count von Zeppelin. I may have made the worst sort of employee at the Zeppelin Airship Works, but Dr. Malvern agrees I will make a much better business partner. We are to build a working model of the Veil to power the BZ-45 touring class airship. Is that not exciting? We may even be able to visit you and Lizzie in Munich during the spring term as part of a test flight.

     I am saving a bit of news for last. We have long known that you need a larger space for your experimental flock. As each generation of chicks is hatched, their housing requirements increase, and I of all people understand your reluctance to separate the members of your flock. But I have heard from my darling Viscount St. Ives that trouble is stirring in my mother's breast over the sheer numbers your dear grandfather is managing on your behalf. Pride of Cornwall though they be, apparently enough chickens are quite enough for Lady Jermyn.

Dr. Malvern and I have been keeping our ears to the ground in this regard, and we may have found a solution. A small house with a large property has recently fallen vacant, only a quarter of a mile from the Carrick Airfield. I suggest that when you are home for Christmas, you might inspect it. The house is sturdy but very much neglected; you may find it useful for offices. It is the property that is attractive—a well drained slope, grassy, and treed at intervals useful for shade in summer. It will require work to make it habitable and organized for a flock, but I must say its location is highly convenient. Vauxhall Gardens is not the most fashionable address. It is still the south bank, after all. But its proximity to our other interests makes it very attractive.

I leave this with you for now. Kiss Lizzie for me, and know that I am

Always your loving
Claire

CHAPTER 1

London

arguerite Polgarth—Maggie to her friends— stood at the freshly painted white gate of the property that now, much to the astonishment of everyone she knew, belonged exclusively to her. She had never owned anything more costly than a good pair of Drosslmayer boots. For all her exhilaration, it was rather frightening to be a landowner of two acres.

"Go on, Maggie, dear." Lady Claire Malvern's soft voice came from behind her. "There is nothing to be afraid of."

"There is if there's rats in the attic, Lady," came eight-year-old Lucy's voice in tones of grim experience.

"There are no rats in *my* attic," Maggie said firmly, and pushed open the gate.

All but one of the people she loved best in the world trooped in after her. The Lady's hand rested lightly in the crook of Dr. Malvern's elbow as she took in the neat roofed houses that would shelter Maggie's flock of prize-winning

Buff Orpington chickens, each house with its own predator-proof yard, some with trees. Each strain of temperament or appearance for which she was testing genetic theories would have its own yard, and soon would be filled with the glorious golden birds so beloved of her grandfather at Gwynn Place.

Lizzie Seacombe, Maggie's cousin, was less interested in the study of genetics that the flock represented and much more interested in the cottage. She and her intended, Lieutenant Tom Terwilliger of the Royal Aeronautics Corps, were inching closer to a wedding date, with a consequent rise in inquiries apropos of nothing. "What do you think of the new water closets, Lady?" and "South-facing windows in the drawing room. On that point I will not be moved" might issue forth in the middle of a conversation about menus or mechanics. The fact that she was no closer to either windows or water closets than the man in the moon did not concern Lizzie at all. She was far-sighted in more ways than one.

And here was the cottage, repaired, reroofed, refitted, and whitewashed until it looked—to Maggie's eyes at least—brand new. As she laid her hand on the door latch, she heard a pounding from inside.

"Are the carpenters still here?" The Lady joined her on the neatly swept sandstone doorstep.

"I thought they were supposed to have finished." Maggie opened the door to see a tall, lanky figure in the act of hanging a picture over the mantel, which was a simple slab of oak. A picture of the woman in the miniature that at this moment hung from a blue ribbon at Maggie's throat.

She gasped, and Jake looked over his shoulder.

"Hullo, Mags," he said. "I didn't think you were coming until teatime."

"We couldn't wait," she said faintly. "What—how—"

"You must blame your brother Claude," the Lady said, taking her hand as Maggie stared wordlessly at the portrait. "We thought to surprise you in your new office. It was Jake's idea to have the portrait painted in a size approaching that of the one Lizzie has of her mother."

"I'm afraid the artist—a friend of Claude's, he is, name of Sisley—took a few liberties with it." Jake, the most self-possessed person Maggie knew, sounded anxious. "If you don't like it, I'll take it down."

She had never seen anything so lovely in her life. The artist had clearly had a good look at the miniature, for the gentle face of her mother was the same. But there the resemblance between the pictures ended, for this portrait was of a woman in a lavender dress, dappled sunlight falling upon her hair and shoulders. She seemed to be sitting in a garden ... or perhaps in a field. It was painted in the Impressionist style that Maggie adored, the dots and dabs of pigment somehow coalescing in a way that was like all the separate instruments in an orchestra combining to produce one magnificent sound.

"Aw, Mags, don't cry." Jake put an arm about her shoulders in a rough hug. "I don't mind that you don't like it. I'll have it out of here in a jiffy."

"No!" she said hoarsely, wiping the tears of joy off her cheeks. "I love it more than anything. Don't you dare touch it."

"Really?" Jake looked as though he thought she was funning him.

"Truly." To convince him, she stretched up and pecked him on the cheek. "Thank you. If Claude were here I'd kiss him, too. I've never received anything that meant so much—except the original." She touched her locket.

He turned scarlet and mumbled something about getting the ladder out of here, and he and it promptly vanished.

"How kind of Jake and your brother." Dr. Malvern regarded the portrait with undisguised admiration, then looked about the empty room. Its plank flooring gleamed with polish, its plaster-over-stone walls whitewashed. Across the hall was a small dining room, equally white and empty.

The Lady walked past her husband into the back, on the heels of Lucy and one of the Alfreds. "Goodness, Maggie, do you plan to cook at your place of business? On one of your trips here, you were pulling all the fittings out. I thought you were going to house chicks in this room or some such."

"I did have the fittings pulled out." Maggie took a breath. She must tell them now, while the truth was staring everyone in the face. "And I had a modern steam cooker put in, as well as plumbing in the water closet. The pipes to the bathing room are connected to the boiler, so it will have the luxury of both hot and cold water."

Lizzie leaped to her own conclusion. "Maggie, you're not going to *live* here, surely."

"I am. There are two bedrooms upstairs, and one of them shall be mine."

"What?" The Lady had gone pale. "Leave Carrick House? Leave us?"

Maggie could not bear to distress the Lady—the one person in all the world besides Lizzie and her grandfather whom she loved the most. She took Claire's hand and that of her cousin, who was still staring at her in disbelief. "I would never leave the flock. Never. We will see each other often. But when the birds come, I cannot trust them to just anyone. I must be here myself."

"But—but how?" Lizzie asked. "We have more than two years left at university in Munich."

Maggie bit her lip. It felt as though she had committed a series of betrayals. The steam cooker was merely the last of them. "I applied to the sciences department at the University of London. And was accepted, upon Uncle Ferdinand's recommendation. I may take my place starting as soon as January." Her voice faltered. "I have not quite made up my mind. Not yet. Though I must very soon."

"Good heavens." Claire turned to Dr. Malvern in appeal. "Andrew, she cannot live here alone."

"No indeed," he agreed. Then, on seeing Maggie's pleated brow and the distress she must be showing as they knocked down all her careful dreams, he went on hastily, "Though she is of age, and I must say that any woman who could pay cash for this property and its improvements out of her own investments is no ordinary woman."

"I think she proved *that* in the English Channel, when she scuttled the French invasion," Lizzie reminded them all. "But whether she *can* is not the point. Whether she *ought* is the question."

Maggie turned away to touch the mantel, smooth with oil and elbow grease. The carpenters, overseen by Jake and Lewis, and periodically by herself on her flying visits since October, had been scrupulous in their work. She would not change a single thing. In fact, now that she was here, in the finished cottage and not the tumbledown wreck it had been, an urgency to wrap the tiny house about her like a shawl was growing inside her breast with every minute that passed.

For her mother's portrait had worked some kind of alchemy … and made a space a home. She wanted to live in it, without delay. To do satisfying work, to find joy in independence, to see what more she might be capable of. To fly the nest, as her chicks did when they were ready to see the world.

Lizzie joined her in front of the cold, pristine fireplace. "What about me, Mags? Please don't leave me alone in Munich."

"Alone?" she said in a low tone. "You have made friends. We both have. You are far from alone at any minute of the day. Besides, we will have holidays at the same time, to spend at Carrick House or in Cornwall."

"It's not the same." Lizzie's eyes held a dawning apprehension that Maggie might really go through with this. "Who will I whisper secrets to late at night? I'll likely get some horrid roommate and we will do nothing but fight. And who will walk with me after dinner in the park? Who will tell me what dreadful taste I have in hats when we go shopping in the Marienplatz?"

Maggie wavered. "Lizzie …"

For she was right. In Munich, with only a few exceptions, they did everything together. They watched each other's backs the way they had done since they were five years old and had plunged into the Thames from a burning airship, to be reborn as the Mopsies. Street sparrows. Pickpockets and thieves.

Until they had made the Lady their mark and everything had changed.

And now everything would change again.

The Lady's gray gaze had not left Maggie's face. She joined them at the hearth and said, "Lizzie, come with me and Dr. Malvern. I want to take a ramble over the property. I believe we can see the airfield from the top of the slope."

"But Lady—"

"Please, Lizzie," she said in the gentle tone that meant there was likely more to the ramble than met the eye.

Lizzie sighed. "All right. I do want to be able to write Tigg a full account. Especially about the boiler."

The three of them walked outside and, like mice when the house is empty, Lucy and Alfred peeped out of the kitchen.

Maggie smiled at them. "Are you going with the Lady?"

"No." Alfred glanced at Lucy as if for confirmation. "We 'ave an offer for you, Maggie, if you'll 'ear us."

"An offer?" Of what might this offer consist? Maggie knew as well as anyone that the two of them had two suits of clothes each, plus a good one for Sundays, and that was the extent of their worldly goods. Surely they had not returned to the thieving ways they had been forced to employ before they came to Carrick House? For that would result in immediate dismissal, and every child there knew it.

Lucy came farther into the room to take her hand confidingly. "If you come to live here, we want to come, too."

Thunderstruck, Maggie stared at her.

As though to stave off a refusal, Alfred leaped in. "We were talking it over back there, and we both agree. If you'll 'ave us, Lucy can keep 'ouse for you, and I shall be your groundskeeper, cleaning out the coops and fixing the enclosures. I know 'ow," he said, as though she had demurred. "Your granddad showed me when we was there in the summer. He said 'imself I were a dab hand."

Maggie doubted that Polgarth the Gwynn Place poultryman had ever said such a thing in his life, but she took the boy's meaning as it had been intended.

"I am honored by your trust," she said carefully. Both faces lit up. "But truly, it would not do. For what would become of your studies, both of you? Your lessons in writing, and arithmetic, and mechanics? Your studies in cookery, Lucy, from Granny Protheroe? And yours in carpentry, Alfred, from Mr. Cooper? For between my studies and my experiments here, it will still be as though I am in Munich. I will not be able to give you your lessons." Her gaze became as stern as ever the Lady's could be. "I will not be a party to any scheme that deprives you both of your education."

Their faces fell. Lucy blinked rapidly to hold back tears. Maggie had meant to be practical, not to make them unhappy. Her own throat tightened. She must repair the situation before Lizzie came back and made it worse.

"There might be a solution," came a male voice from the doorway in its familiar Scots Cockney accents.

Maggie turned as Jake stepped into the room, the long beam of winter sunlight falling around him. Her house was freezing cold with no fire in the hearth or water in the boiler, but they had bundled up in wool coats and mittens for this excursion. And emotion kept a person warm, that was certain.

He joined them, his head only six inches or so from the black beams of oak that supported the ceiling. "We must look at the situation in steps," he said. "Like igniting the Lady's landau, aye? First one thing, and then the next, and you can't mix them up because then it won't work."

"And you know these steps?" Maggie hardly knew whether to be grateful or annoyed at this intrusion into a decision that ought to be hers alone.

"I don't know much of anything," he admitted with a glance at her from under his shaggy hair, "but I do make my living as a navigator. I'm able to see my way from one place to another. Will you hear me out?"

"Oh yes," little Lucy said, her eyes shining. She admired Jake enormously, though she was a tiny bit afraid of him.

Any sensible person would be.

"Maggie?" Jake persisted.

"Can I stop you?" she asked quizzically, and he laughed.

"You know I would never do anything to displease you," he said. "Never, Mags."

She turned away to gaze once more at her mother's portrait. "All right, then. I'm listening."

"Step one," Jake said. "You go to university here."

"Agreed," she said to the portrait.

"Step two, the children continue their lessons in the mornings with Vicar Lemon, as usual. After lunch on every second day, they come here to help you as they've already said they would. On the other days, they continue their studies with Granny and Mr. Cooper."

Maggie was silent. With the younger children, afternoons at Carrick House were spent in walks to the park for exercise, or to places such as the Museum of Natural History for real illustrations of what they had learned. In Lucy's case, she spent the afternoons with Granny Protheroe, and Alfred with the carpenter. The Lady and Dr. Malvern repaired to their laboratory in Orpington Close to work.

It was a system of education that had evolved from the days when the Lady had been their main instructress, with Maggie as her assistant. It worked well. Did she really have the right to interrupt it for Lucy and Alfred, even if it was their own suggestion?

"Where will we sleep?" Alfred wanted to know.

"Here, of course," Jake said. "That way, Maggie is not left alone, and anyone at the airfield may take you to Carrick House in the jalopy in the morning. Getting back again, mind you, is your own nevermind."

"You seem to have this all thought out," Maggie said, again caught between gratitude and annoyance. "Have the three of you been conspiring since the autumn?"

"No indeed." Lucy looked shocked.

"I thought about it as I was putting away the ladder," Jake confessed. "It seems a workable plan. The only fact that may not be reasoned away is that you cannot stay here alone."

"I—I must talk it over with the Lady," Maggie said with a shake of her head. "It is all too new. I must say I never thought to have any of the children here. But I do like the idea, if we can maintain a regular system of study."

"Hurrah!" Alfred threw his cap in the air, then caught it and jammed it back on his head. Maggie couldn't blame him. It was really very cold—the frost had not even melted off the grass, and it was well past noon.

"Don't go taking it for granted yet." Jake gripped the boy's shoulder while Alfred bravely tried not to squirm. "It's far from settled, and there's still Lizzie to deal with."

"I will handle my cousin," Maggie said.

The last thing she needed was for Lizzie and Jake to get into a knock-down-drag-out. These days, she wouldn't want to bet on who would win.

CHAPTER 2

*J*ake sometimes thought of himself as quite the man about town. He had his old room at Carrick House for when he was in London. He had his cabin in the crew's quarters aboard *Swan*, of course, for longer voyages. Captain Lady Alice Hollys did not require his services for short hauls, for she was as happy to employ Captain Sir Ian as navigator as that gentleman was to have her to himself. Benny Stringfellow, erstwhile midshipman and now gunner second class, was all the crew they needed for a run to Bristol or Edinburgh, and Charlie, of course, always went as cook. Finally, should all the bedrooms at Carrick House be full, Lewis assured him of a bed in the owner's private rooms at the Gaius Club should at any time he need one.

It was all very well for a career aeronaut like himself, with excellent prospects in life, to have his choices. But somehow, for a young lady such as Maggie to have similar choices … well, it made Jake uneasy, it did. And it was not a matter of a double standard.

"It's just that she's on the south bank," he said gloomily to Snouts the next day. "What was the Lady thinking, to encourage her to purchase there?"

He, his half-brother, and Lewis Protheroe were taking tea in the parlor in the absence of the Lady and Dr. Malvern. Between mouthfuls of fruitcake and cheese, they were talking over this sensational change looming in the future of their comfortable household.

"The Cudgel is dead," Snouts said around his cake. "That's something."

"But I've heard someone has already stepped into that arch-rogue's shoes," Jake pointed out. "If Maggie is close at hand, they may come for her to get at the Lady. Make a big splash to begin."

"Can you not put a night watchman on the cottage, as you have on the airfield?" Lewis asked.

"We could," Jake allowed. "Until Maggie found out about it. She wouldn't be best pleased, I'll tell you. She'd likely shoot the watchman thinking he was a scout for one of the gangs."

"Pity one of us can't stay with her," Lewis said on a sigh.

Snouts snorted at the ludicrous idea of any of them, family though they were, sleeping unchaperoned in the home of a single woman. "We may be as brothers to her, but the fact is, we're not," he said. "Imagine what the Lady would say."

"We're just going to have to talk Maggie out of it," Lewis said for at least the third time since tea had come in.

"I don't see how," Jake said. "You should have seen her. She's attached to the place already. We could barely convince her to come away. She was like a winkle in its shell, clinging for all she was worth and insisting the place had to be named before we left."

"I can hardly blame the lass," Snouts said after he had contemplated this vivid image. "We three have places where we're in positions of authority. What do the girls have?"

"May I remind you, you relic of a bygone age, that Maggie and Lizzie own one third each of the Seacombe Steamship Company, and that Lizzie will take over its management as soon as she graduates?" Lewis's eyes crinkled with amusement. "Maggie has rather more than we tend to think. The purchase of that cottage has not put a dent in her fortune. She paid cash for it out of her own investments."

All too true. And Lewis would know, for he advised them all in financial matters. Even the Lady and Dr. Malvern.

Maggie was so modest and quietly ambitious in her studies that Jake tended to forget that even if she were to look upon him as more than a brother, despite their shared past, she was as far above him as the rooks dipping and swinging in the sky.

For she was not only easy on the eyes, she was an heiress of the kind that would bring suitors running the moment she lifted her head and looked about her. Why, see what had happened last Christmas, when those blasted Meriwether-Astor brothers had imposed upon them. Both of them had taken one look at Maggie and decided to pursue her. It was only her own good sense that had got rid of them … with a little pressure brought to bear by the Lady and the other inhabitants of Carrick House.

Jake was just about to ask Lewis if he had any other indigent relatives of the sort that might make a suitable chaperone at the little cottage, when the front door opened and Maggie, Sophie, and Lucy came in from their walk.

Maggie saw the young men in the study and stopped on

the threshold to unpin her hat. "Is the tea still hot, or have you lot drunk it all? I declare my fingers have turned to ice."

"I'll put the kettle on." Lucy and Sophie scampered away with the cooling teapot, unbuttoning coats as they went.

Jake blinked at Maggie. She looked as though someone had lit a flame behind her eyes. "What's happened, Mags? Do you have news for us?"

Laughing, she nodded. "We have been up to London University on the steambus. I've accepted the place in the sciences department. Just in time, too, for term begins the second week of January."

Only three weeks, and everything would be different.

"So you've decided, then." Snouts rose to take her coat, and went out into the vestibule to hang it up. "Does Lizzie know?"

"Not yet." Maggie took a piece of cake … and Snouts's comfortable chair. "I'm not looking forward to it. We did talk for a long while last night, but she was not reconciled to the idea."

Jake was not reconciled to it, either, but that did not prevent his saying, "She's a fine one to talk. As soon as Tigg puts the ring on her finger she'll be off billing and cooing in a little dovecote of her own, and sparing not a thought for you."

"Exactly what I said last night." Maggie licked marzipan off her fingers. "It did no good at all. I am in her bad books, for true. But there is no going back now."

Jake could not seem to drag his gaze from her. Wordlessly, he handed her a napkin, and when she took it with a smile, he subsided into the depths of his chair feeling like all kinds of a villain.

He must not look at Maggie's mouth. Or her eyes. Or think of her in any other way but that of sister. For sister was what she was and ever could be. Sister—companion—friend. The most stalwart and brave a man could ask for.

He ought to be on his knees in gratitude to have that much. He was, truly—desperately grateful. He could not jeopardize her regard by so much as a glance. He must squash these unwelcome thoughts back into the Pandora's box from whence they had come with such violence that they never surfaced again.

THE FRONT DOOR slammed and boot heels clacked across the vestibule. The three young men and Maggie looked around as one, to see Lizzie in the doorway, crackling with temper.

"I hope you're pleased," she snapped at Maggie. "They haven't got a place for me at London University and now I have to go back to Munich all by myself."

Maggie's mouth fell open. Lizzie had applied for a place? Just now?

Snouts was the only one with the courage to speak. "Did you *want* a place there?"

"Not until yesterday, I didn't." Lizzie glared at him as though it were all his fault. Maggie knew perfectly well at whom her anger was really directed. "But I'm not going to spend the next two and a half years in Germany while the rest of you are having a lark over here without me."

"Studying is hardly a lark," Lewis said. "Neither is managing one's business."

"You know what I mean." And she stamped a boot for good measure.

"You're lucky the Lady isn't here," came a treble voice from behind her, and Lucy swerved into the room with the teapot in both hands, protected by a caddy. "She wouldn't like you doing that."

Defiantly, Lizzie stamped again.

"All right, missy." Jake got to his feet to take the pot and give Lizzie what for. "Take your temper outside if you can't be a better example."

Her cheeks red, tears standing in her eyes, Lizzie let out a growl of frustration and ran upstairs, every heavy footfall an accusation.

With a sigh, Maggie filled two cups and put milk in both. "I had better talk to her."

"Give her a few minutes," Lewis advised. "She's likely to fling the cup at you. Shame to waste it."

But Maggie knew her cousin better than that. Brave, outspoken, and passionate she might be, but Lizzie was never petty. And she certainly had china enough on her mind these days that she was more likely to turn the cup over to see its maker than throw it.

No matter how much her target grieved and angered her.

She added cake to the saucers and carried them upstairs. "I brought you some tea." Maggie bumped the door of their room closed with her hip and set the offering down on the low dresser under the window between their two beds. Then she fished her handkerchief out of her sleeve and handed it to her cousin as she sat beside her on the coverlet.

Lizzie blew her nose, wiped her face, and finally picked up the tea and took a sip. "I don't mean to be a shrieking harridan."

"I know," Maggie said gently. "It is good practice, though,

for when you are Mrs. Lieutenant Terwilliger and the fish-monger tries to cheat you at the market."

Lizzie snickered into her teacup. "Forgive me?"

"Of course." Maggie sipped her own tea. "You applied for a place next autumn, though, didn't you? Coming in as a third year?"

"I did. So it is only for nine months that I am to be relegated to outer darkness. That is some improvement, I suppose."

"Munich is hardly outer darkness. Why, you might invite Katrina Grünwald to be your roommate. Goodness knows we are her only friends, and she is awfully kind despite her terrifying brain."

"Perhaps I will. But oh, Mags." Lizzie laid her head on Maggie's shoulder. "It won't be the same without you."

"Think of me in a new university where I know no one," Maggie said, a little bleakly. "At least you have all our friends, and the professors know you."

"You may go to your own home at night," Lizzie countered. "And Carrick House too."

"There is no genetics program at London University." This had been a shocking drawback. The only thing to improve it was that they would allow her one self-managed course of study. Other than that, her official degree would be in Applied Biology.

"You will invent one based on the eighteen months you've been studying already. And—" Lizzie sat up. "You might arrange a tutorship with Professor Schaden. The University of Bavaria is always wittering on about building links between institutions, and thus between nations. You might hold their feet to the fire and insist on continuing your classes by tube, under his supervision."

"What a good idea." With one arm, Maggie hugged her. "You see? Nine months will flash by in a moment, and then everything will be back to normal. You'll see."

Lizzie's gaze turned dreamy. "Perhaps this will be better after all. For if I am here, then I will have two years to look about me for a little nest, won't I?"

The Lady would not permit Lizzie and Tigg to marry until she had finished her degree. In Lizzie's mind, this only gave her time to prepare. She would be the most prepared aeronaut's bride the Corps had ever seen.

"How can you, when Tigg could be posted anywhere?" Maggie pointed out. "There is no point in finding a nest here if he is posted to St. Michael's Mount. Or Scotland. Or wherever else the Dunsmuirs require him. You might find yourself nesting in a mine north of Edmonton."

Lizzie shivered. "Don't remind me. Remember how cold it was? And that man who said the airships had to be away before the first snow, or the gas bags would contract and they couldn't fly?"

Maggie remembered all too well. "Speaking of flying, what do you think of Orpington Cottage as a name for my little nest?"

"Too long to paint on a sign." Lizzie turned her attention to her slice of cake. "Gull Cottage?"

"Too great a reminder of cleaning up after birds."

"Never mind birds, then. Something from the land. Primrose Cottage?"

"Did you see primroses?" Maggie asked in some surprise. How could anything come up in a December so cold?

"No, but it sounds pretty. And you could plant some." Lizzie turned over her saucer to look at the maker. "Royal Morvoren. I should have known."

"I like the roses. Rose Cottage?"

"There are thousands of houses in England called Rose Cottage," Lizzie informed her. "But you ought to have a rambling rose over the door, like the one your Aunt Tressa has. It's so welcoming."

Maggie added one to her mental list. Then— "Goodness me, Liz, never mind flowers. If I am to move into the cottage in three weeks, I must have furniture!"

"Excellent." Lizzie's eyes lit up. "Let us speak to the Lady at once, and make plans to go shopping."

"For *me*, Liz."

Lizzie waved a hand. "Of course, for you. But you may be certain I will be making a list alongside you … for I must be prepared, mustn't I, when the time comes?"

CHAPTER 3

*I*t took Claire until well after dinner to reconcile herself to the ripple effect of her sending Maggie that letter back in the autumn. A new cottage bought ... a university program abandoned and a new one taken up ... a cousin left to go on alone ... long-cherished plans set aside.

That such a small thing could cause such upsets in their lives!

"The next time I am tempted to meddle in the Mopsies' affairs," she said to Andrew as they cuddled on the sofa in the parlor, "throw yourself in front of me bodily and bar the door."

"As if I could prevent you doing a single thing you had set your mind to," he scoffed, his arm comfortably around her shoulders. "Rest assured that if Maggie had not been interested in your suggestion, none of this would have come about. She is a young lady who knows her own mind."

"And knows how to achieve what she sets out to do," Jake said from the hearth rug in front of them, where he was stretched out like a species of lanky cat.

As though summoned from upstairs, Maggie entered the parlor with a list in one hand and a pencil in the other. "Lady, will it be all right if I take my bed to the cottage? Or would you prefer it stay here for guests, and I purchase my own?"

"Having the two beds together in that room is useful for guests," Claire said thoughtfully, "but it is yours. Which should you prefer?"

"I should like to get one of those lovely wrought-iron bedsteads that are so popular now."

"Snouts can make you one at the manufactory," Jake said. "They employ ironmasters there who can work iron the way glassmakers do glass, in filigree and all sorts of fanciful shapes."

"Oh, I couldn't ask him to—" She glanced anxiously at Snouts, who was playing cards with Lizzie, Lewis, and one of the Alfreds.

"You have only to think of a pattern you'd like," Snouts said with a grand bow, "and it is done."

With a smile, Maggie made a tick on her list.

"You might hunt about up in the attics," Claire suggested. "Anything up there is fair game. Oh!" She was struck by a sudden thought. "We ought to fly down to Gwynn Place. There is four hundred years' worth of clobber in the attics there. It would be like Vauxhall Market for you, only without the frost. Or the pickpockets."

For an unguarded moment, Maggie's face registered dismay at the thought of furnishing her home with four-hundred-year-old clobber. Then her natural humility of spirit —and her practicality—erased it. "I would like that very much, Lady. How soon might we go?"

Claire pulled her down on the sofa next to her. "There are

some fine pieces up there from my grandmother's time, during the Tinkering Prince's regency. I remember with particular admiration a sideboard that changed shape depending on the size of the space it occupied. It horrified my mother. No one has looked at any of it in two generations at least. Lady Jermyn cannot object if my darling Viscount does not—and you know how he loves you."

If Maggie had quailed at the thought of asking Lady Jermyn for so much as a bone button, the thought of little Nicholas made her eyes sparkle.

"Andrew, does Thursday suit for a trip to Cornwall?" Claire asked her husband.

He settled her more comfortably against his side. "Have we any engagements?"

"None that we cannot put off."

"I will check the weather stations," Jake offered, "and navigate for you, if you like."

"I should be delighted." Claire smiled at him. Though she could navigate the familiar route with one eye closed, if Jake wanted to be among their number, she would never refuse him.

"We ought to bring crates," Maggie said, making another note. "For if we make the effort of flying down, we ought to bring some of the flock back, and settle them in their new home."

Alfred laid down his cards, and Lewis whooped in triumph as he won. "I'll build you a dozen at the carpentry shop, then, shall I?" the boy asked. "Since the birds are to be my responsibility?"

"Thank you, Alfred." He beamed at Claire's approval and Maggie's thanks, and abandoned his cards to run upstairs, where sounds of thumping told Claire he was looking for his valise in the closet.

"Are you certain, Lady?" Maggie asked. "I do not wish to throw the whole household into a furor simply because I require furniture. I could simply buy something at the warehouses and have it delivered."

"Are we not to go shopping?" Lizzie said in falling tones of disappointment, collecting the cards together. "At all?"

"Of course," Claire assured her. "One still must have plates to eat from, and kettles to cook in. But for the larger items, unless Maggie's tastes are such that she is set on one particular thing, it seems logical to use what we already possess."

"I agree." Maggie nodded. "I should like a memento or two of Gwynn Place. Some of my happiest days have been spent there. If there is a dining-room table to be had, I will take it, even if it is four hundred years old."

And so it was settled. On Thursday, the traveling party set out from Carrick House in the landau and the jalopy, a dozen crates freshly assembled by Alfred tied on the cover of the latter in a teetering stack. They lifted within the hour, each member of the party except perhaps Lucy familiar with his or her duties on ropes or in the gondola.

Four hours later, the West Country scrolled away beneath the hull, every fold of field and hedge, every watercourse and cove familiar to Claire from many flights such as this one. And when the icy blue of the Carrick Roads came into view, she could not help the warm glow of homecoming.

Gwynn Place was her home no longer. In point of fact, on a voyage *Athena* herself was her home. But as Andrew took her hand, it was clear that he also understood. For wherever they were together, there was their home.

~

YOUNG NICHOLAS, Viscount St. Ives, waited in one of the dormant fields at Gwynn Place, along with a tall individual whose dress told Jake he was likely the boy's tutor, ready to tie *Athena's* bow line to the tree they typically used. When the gangway ratcheted out to touch the earth, Jake and Alfred disembarked to see to the other ropes, while Nicholas flew into his sister's arms.

"Clary! How happy I am to see you! Mama was so surprised at your tube. Can you stay for a long time?"

Laughing, the Lady hugged him, gave him two more kisses, then passed him to Dr. Malvern for a second round of both. "I am afraid this is quite literally a flying visit. But we will make the most of it, will we not?"

Nicholas nodded. The little lord was always willing to look at a glass half full. "Clary, Dr. Malvern, Maggie—come and be introduced. May I present my tutor, Mr. Alden Dean. He was away from Gwynn Place the last time you were here."

Jake kept an eye on the proceedings as he tied the ship down to her stakes, then he and Alfred joined the little group in time for Mr. Dean to bow to Maggie.

"Miss Polgarth, how do you do? I have heard so much of you from your grandfather I feel as though I know you already."

Jake frowned at this familiarity.

Maggie dipped a pretty curtsey, apparently unaffected by either familiarity or frown. "I am afraid, sir, that love makes my grandfather a very poor judge where I am concerned."

"I am certain that is not the case," he said gallantly.

Stepping forward, Jake caught the Lady's eye, and she said

smoothly, before Mr. Dean could spout any more nonsense, "Mr. Dean, this is Jake Fletcher McTavish, navigator in the Royal Aeronautic Corps, and my ward, Alfred Shore."

"I am pleased to make your acquaintance, sirs," the young man said pleasantly. Then, to Nicholas, he said, "Come, my lord. We must not keep your lady mother waiting for a first glimpse of her daughter."

Nicholas obligingly led the way, clinging to the Lady's hand and chattering in high spirits. This left Mr. Dean to fall in next to Maggie—or it would have, if Dr. Malvern had not stepped up to engage him in conversation about his theories of private education.

Dr. Malvern was a prince among men.

Jake stalked along the path to the orchard, and from there to the great house, at Maggie's side. He was not normally tongue-tied, but he supposed she would not appreciate a lecture about the dangers of being alone with such a forward individual, educated gentleman or not. Jake might come across as a brother, but he would not risk sounding like a jealous suitor for anything.

The result was that as they passed through the gate in the wall that led to the wide lawns and the front of the house, Maggie glanced at him curiously. "Are you well, Jake? You seem awfully quiet."

He thought quickly. "I'm just enjoying being here again."

Her smile was so beautiful he lost his train of thought. "I am, too. I am going to pay my respects to Sir Richard and Lady Jermyn, and then escape to Grandfather's cottage. I have no doubt he knows we are coming, and has been watching the skies all afternoon."

"Would you like me to come with you?"

This time her smile warmed him all the way to his toes. "At any other time, in any other place but this one, I would say yes without hesitation. But I want it to be just the two of us. I can make Grandfather's tea. And see Aunt Tressa. You understand, don't you?"

"If I had family like yours, I would do the same," he admitted.

"You do have family," she told him quietly as they entered the hall to find Sir Richard and his wife waiting for them. "You have us."

Which did not result in the warm, uplifted feeling Maggie had clearly intended. Yet another reminder that she saw him merely as a brother rather cast him into the dumps. As the others trooped into the drawing room for sherry and cake, and she slipped away, it seemed to Jake as though she took the sunshine with her.

The skies had been clear and icy cold as they sailed through them earlier, the winter equinox just past. The sun sinking now in a butter-yellow sky lent no warmth. And the pleasant, smiling young man who approached him did nothing to improve the prospect.

"Miss Polgarth did not come in?"

"She has gone to see her grandfather and auntie." Jake's tone conveyed his surprise that this needed to be explained. "She would not delay her errand by more than a few minutes."

"A pleasure for them and a loss for us."

For the love of heaven, did the man have a gallantry for every word a person said?

"Do you know the young lady well?"

Jake felt his spine tingle with the urge to square up and

swing. He pushed the feeling down. "Aye, we have known one another since I was eight and she five."

"Have you?" Mr. Dean looked surprised. "Are your families acquainted?"

"You might say so. We were Lady Claire's wards as children, much as Alfred is now."

"Remarkable." He glanced at the Lady. "Her ladyship does not look much older than you, to have such responsibility."

"Happiness will keep a person looking well, I hear." It was something the Lady had said once, and it seemed appropriate now. "And now that we are older, and embarking on our careers, we share the responsibility for the younger ones."

"Miss Polgarth, I understand, is at university?"

"Mr. Dean, I do not like to discuss Miss Polgarth behind her back," Jake said pleasantly, in his most gentlemanly tones. The tones he had developed by studying Dr. Malvern and the way he spoke. "Perhaps you ought to put your questions to her."

"Oh, I shall indeed," Mr. Dean said with some warmth, as though Jake had given him permission to pay his addresses to Maggie.

Which Jake most certainly had not.

"I shall ask her to go in to dinner with me," the man said happily, and strolled away to join Dr. Malvern and Sir Richard.

If Jake could have put a fist through the window, he would have.

Dinner was delicious, but for Jake it was an unmitigated failure. Watching Maggie laughing and talking with the educated man made the deep, savory meat pie turn to sawdust in his mouth. The rest of the evening fared no better, to the point where Jake felt the company would thank him if he just went away to his cabin on *Athena*.

But instead of going to bed, there was a task he must complete in privacy. A moonglobe in one hand, he took a shovel from the shed in the kitchen garden and loped down the lane to the snug cottage of Maggie's grandfather, Polgarth the poultryman.

At his knock, the old man answered, his white hair backlit to gold by the light of the old-fashioned oil lamps. "Why, Mr. McTavish. Come in."

"I will not keep you, Mr. Polgarth," Jake said hastily. "I only wanted your permission for something. Something important to me."

Polgarth pulled a heavy shawl from a peg and wrapped it about himself as he stepped outside. "I might think you wanted permission to court my granddaughter, but I see by your shovel you have come on a different errand."

Jake's cold fingers lost hold of the shovel, and it clattered to the flagged path.

"Careful, lad." Polgarth handed it back to him. "I guessed wrong. No harm done."

"I—no—how in heaven's name did—I mean, no, it's not about that."

"I have known you for a handful of years, lad. I've seen you with Maggie, and she with you. Of all the young men who have come down here with my young lady Claire, I would sooner trust my granddaughter to you than any."

Jake lost his breath. "I don't—I never—she would never—"

"That is as may be," the old man said, unperturbed at having upended Jake's world in only a few sentences. "Now then, what do you plan to dig up? I can *almost* guarantee there is no smuggler's cache in my garden."

Jake took a moment to breathe and collect his flapping thoughts. "A holly sapling, sir."

"To what purpose?" Polgarth's tone was mystified.

Perhaps he had been expecting Jake to have to bury a body. In the case of Alden Dean, the thought was tempting. "For Maggie. For her new home, I mean."

"Ah." The older man's voice held understanding now. "The country people say that holly is a protective tree. Prickly on the outside, and like to wound the careless, but strong and durable. They used to make weapons of the wood, you know, back when Cornwall was the home of the little dark ones. But in the language of flowers that Maggie's mother used to speak, it meant both *protection* and *domestic happiness*."

"Does it indeed, sir," Jake said. He had not known any of this. He'd merely wanted to give Maggie something from her grandfather's garden. Something that would last, and be good to look at out of her window in the winter. "I would like to plant it by her gate. As a present for Twelfth Night, and a housewarming gift."

"You go right ahead. I assume you've chosen your tree?"

"I have, sir. I saw the very one on my way in."

"Then you have my permission."

"Thank you, sir." Jake hefted the shovel and turned away.

"For that, and the other thing."

Jake nearly tripped and fell into a lavender plant, pruned and sleeping for winter. But before he could reply, Polgarth had gone into the house and closed the door.

The ground was hard, and Jake was sweating by the time he got the sapling dug up and a length of burlap wrapped about its roots. He wrapped another about its prickly branches. The little tree might only come up to his chest, but already it was serious about its task of protection.

Then, back on *Athena*, he concealed it in his cabin, with a coat hung over a hook on top of it. The boiler kept the living quarters tolerably warm, so it would be safe from freezing. Jake washed and climbed into his sleeping cupboard, satisfied with his night's work. The silence of the country closed around him. At least out in the field he would no longer hear the sound of Alden Dean's voice.

Only Polgarth's, saying the words aloud that Jake had never dared speak, or even think.

He pulled the coverlet over his head. But it could not be said that his slumbers were particularly restful.

CHAPTER 4

*I*n the morning, as far as Jake was concerned, the prospect was a little brighter, for the young viscount had his lessons and Mr. Dean had perforce to administer them. As bleary as he was, that was a blessing. The day's task was to storm the attics on Maggie's behalf. After breakfast, the Lady led their exploratory party up four flights of stairs to the servants' quarters, and then up a last steep flight of iron steps to the attics.

"You were not in the room last night, Jake, when my mother realized that she was about to be rid of the Tinkering Prince's articulated sideboard," the Lady said over her shoulder, laughter in her voice, as they climbed. "She could not contain her joy, and anything else we wanted for Maggie's cottage was not too high a price to pay for its disposal."

"I am glad to hear it," he said. "But I'm wondering about these stairs, Lady. Will the thing telescope itself into one of our pockets so we may carry it down?"

The Lady turned the key in the door at the top, and set her shoulder to it when it would not open easily. She gave way to her husband, who shoved it open with one firm blow, and they all passed through.

"I am afraid we will need to disassemble it," she said when they were all in the wide attic, illuminated by the dormer windows in the roof and the moonglobes they had brought with them. "That, or rope it out a window and lower it to the ground with *Athena*'s help."

"Dissasembly," Jake suggested, and Dr. Malvern nodded his agreement. "But I am sure Maggie would like to see it work before we take it apart. I know I would."

The Lady walked over to a sheet covering something whose shape resembled that of a model train, which told Jake no one had touched it since she had been a girl living here. "We must give it a wall."

"There isn't one," Alfred said. For the walls were stacked high with clobber—shelves, dress forms, tennis rackets and cricket bats, a bowl-shaped object that Jake realized was a coracle, trunks filled with clothing and quilts. Furniture lay under sheets, chairs stacked one upon another, and while it seemed someone might come up once a year to clear out the spiderwebs and some of the dust, there was still a goodly amount of both.

"The door?" Dr. Malvern suggested. "We must move it over there anyway."

The Lady pulled off the sheet to reveal a series of boxes lying on the floor. They were very nice boxes, mind you, of some glossy black wood inlaid with a lighter wood in a kind of parquet of diamonds inside squares.

"That … is a sideboard?" Maggie said. "Are you certain those are not packing boxes for china?"

"Quite certain." The Lady laid down the sheet, moved the

box at one end, and pointed it at the door. Then she wound a key in the box and stepped back.

Jake leaned in to watch it. Nothing happened.

Then a whirring sound commenced and he nearly jumped out of his skin when the boxes began to tumble toward the door. They crossed the dusty floor on the sheet, their latches connecting and reconnecting as they went, turning and tumbling in a dignified, controlled manner. When they reached the door, they climbed upon one another until they formed a vertical rectangle to match the space they had been allotted.

"Jupiter," Dr. Malvern said, his eyes wide. "What an extraordinary contraption."

Maggie clapped her hands in delight. "I must have it. It is unique and useful and utterly wonderful."

"But why does your mother dislike it so, Lady?" Jake finally found his voice, since the sideboard appeared content to be a dresser for the time being. He was keeping his eye on it, though.

"She does not like its lifelike movement," the Lady said. "I suspect it is for the same reason she dislikes masquerades, and harlequins, and mummers. They purport to be what they are not."

Dr. Malvern was opening drawers in the dresser and examining its catches and gears. "Remarkable the mind that composed this," he murmured. "What a time it was for invention under the Tinkering Prince! The more silly and wonderful, the better. I should not wonder if it could take itself downstairs without human assistance at all."

"But then it would be scratched on those iron steps, and

SHELLEY ADINA

that I will not allow," Maggie said firmly. "We will carry it. Lady, what other marvels have you up here?"

Nearly seven hours of dusty labor later, with the help of two footmen and a wagon from the home farm, they had loaded Maggie's household goods into *Athena*'s hold and collapsed in her saloon like so many marionettes with cut strings.

Nicholas and Alden Dean had joined them for the last load, and one would think his adorable lordship had arranged the whole enterprise, so pleased was he to be able to help.

"A dining table and six chairs left here by one of my great-aunts Beaton," he said, counting on his fingers. "The articulated sideboard—though I shall miss it. I should have liked to play with it."

"Our mother would die before she allowed that," the Lady said, accepting a glass of sherry from her husband. "One Regency couch, one sofa, and two wingback chairs belonging to my paternal grandmother," she went on, continuing the count.

"A small Turkey rug brought home on his travels by the second Viscount," Nicholas said, turning down another finger. "Clary, is he the one with the sword, or the one with the eye patch?"

"Eye patch," his sister said. "He was beset by pirates off the coast of Zanzibar. Before the portrait was painted. Much to his lady wife's dismay."

"And a set of silver," his lordship concluded, "but no one knows where it comes from. I do not like it, Maggie. Who would want to eat with dirty black knives and spoons?"

"They will be neither dirty nor black once I have polished them," Maggie told him affectionately. "They must be two hundred years old. Did you see the handles? They are figures, like chess pieces."

"You will certainly have an unusual household," Mr. Dean said. He took a cautious sip of his sherry, as though he expected to be intoxicated by a single mouthful. "To what does all this activity tend? Is there a wedding in the offing?"

Maggie looked a little confused. "My cousin is engaged to be married, but she is in London. Did you meet her when she was down to Penzance at Christmas?"

"I referred to the possibility of yours, Miss Polgarth."

Maggie laughed. "No, indeed. I am taking up residence in my own cottage, sir, so that I may establish my experimental flock as part of my degree in Applied Biology."

It took him a moment to absorb all these facts. "Applied Biology?" Then, "Your own cottage?"

"Bought with her own money," Alfred said with pride. "I am to assist her with the flock."

Mr. Dean lowered his glass. "A woman of independent means, then?"

"Quite." Jake felt himself blowing up from the inside, like one of those toads in the Wild West that emitted a bass croak from their holes in the mud. "Why such surprise? Many young ladies of our acquaintance are capable of supporting themselves."

"They may be capable of it," the young man said, "but few actually engage in it. Surely, Miss Polgarth, you are not to live alone?"

"No," Maggie said. "Alfred will be with me, once we make arrangements for his education, and Lucy will help me keep house. Fortunately, I like to cook, so there is no difficulty there. I have nowhere for a cook to sleep in any case. The cottage has only six rooms. Five, really, for my study upstairs is more of a loft."

"You will be taking many meals with us at Carrick House, I hope," the Lady said with a smile.

Mr. Dean was looking from one to the other in growing dismay. "Am I to understand, Lady Claire, that you approve this plan?"

"I admit it surprised me a little when Maggie first broached it, but the more we loaded into the hold this afternoon, the more pleased I became. Creating a home is such fun, is it not?"

Mr. Dean did not look as though this was his particular definition of fun. He did not look as though he was having any fun at all.

Jake subsided into his glass of sherry with a smile, and relaxed for the first time since they had moored.

BEFORE THIS, Maggie had only moved twice, if you didn't count the perpetual search for a dry, safe squat in the early days. The first real move had been very simple—from Toll Cottage to Carrick House, where the sum total of the Mopsies' belongings could be carried in a basket—and that included two hens. The second had been moving to the Continent for university last year. But nothing was quite so momentous as preparing to move into her very own home.

First, the flock must be settled, before any thought could be given to herself. On their return from Gwynn Place, she supervised the chickens' release into the enclosure closest to the cottage, Alfred anxiously shepherding each pair of birds out of their crates and into the grass. It was not until the alpha hen of the group marched up the ramp into the house and deigned to roost under its eaves did he let out a long breath of relief.

"They'll settle now," he confided to Maggie, who smothered a smile so as not to wound his dignity. "I wasn't sure what I should do if they took off and run."

Then at last Maggie could turn her attention to her own situation. In came the dining table and chairs. The articulated sideboard made itself at home along the wall opposite the window, within easy distance of the table. Down went the second viscount's Turkey rug in the parlor. The sofas and chairs were arranged upon it in a way that welcomed friends and encouraged conversation … and hid the worn spots. The regency sofa went upstairs into her study, where her desk from Carrick House had already been situated.

Maggie could hardly wait to get her hands on some silver polish. But in its absence, the peculiar set of silver rested in its battered box in one of the segments of the sideboard.

She possessed only one pot for cooking and a cast-iron frying pan, but as Lizzie said, "That is all the more reason for us to visit the shops and warehouses. For we must have linens, and curtains too. If you will not put them in your hope chest, like any other young lady, then we must busy ourselves. I won't have you visiting the rag-pickers."

"Nor do I wish to," she assured her cousin. "Those days are gone forever, and good riddance."

Over the next several days, she found it soothing to hemstitch linens in spare moments—dish towels, sheets, tablecloths. Lizzie was right. Most girls made such things while they waited for their prince to come. But Maggie had no need of that mythical creature. She was perfectly happy to create a home for herself and the two children without benefit of a lord of the manor.

For now, at least. Life was too full and too interesting to spend it as some of the girls at university did, dashing from ball to card party to theatre in order to meet as many men as possible. She often wondered when they found time to study. There would be no M.R.S. degree for her. She was determined to have the miles of hemstitching done by the time term began—and to move in by Twelfth Night.

"Maggie," Lucy said, on tiptoe at the window, "here comes the Lady in the steam landau, and a gentleman with her."

"Not Doctor Malvern?" Lizzie put aside the pillowcase that she was trimming with crocheted lace—the latter a gift from Granny Protheroe.

"No, I've never seen him before."

In a moment the mystery was solved, as Mr. Alden Dean removed his top hat, ducked under the lintel, and followed the Lady in.

"Look who is in London, visiting friends," the Lady said cheerfully. "Mr. Dean begged me to show him the cottage, so I believe we have the honor of being your very first callers, Maggie."

"It is I who am honored." Maggie dipped a curtsey. "How do you do, Mr. Dean? You know my cousin Elizabeth?"

The gentleman bowed. "I have that pleasure. How do you do, Miss Seacombe?"

"Very well, thank you." Lizzie could not leave off gazing between him and Maggie, as though she were trying to solve an equation: one plus one equals two. Well, Maggie would soon disabuse her of that notion. Engaged women were far too apt to want everyone about them to enjoy a similar state.

"And this is Lucy," Maggie said, as the girl curtseyed. "She did not come to Gwynn Place with us last week. Lucy, this is Viscount St. Ives's tutor, Mr. Alden Dean."

"Good day, sir," Lucy said. Then, to Maggie, "I'll get the tea, shall I?"

"Thank you—we have a teapot?"

"I brought the brown one from Carrick House today."

"And I brought cake," the Lady said, extracting a tin from her bag. "Granny Protheroe would have sent the entire contents of the pantry had I not forestalled her. She is convinced you will starve on your own."

"We do not even live here yet, but we have not starved," Maggie said with a smile. "Each time we come, Lucy and Alfred make sure something new is added to our pantry. This morning it was the teapot. Yesterday it was potatoes and carrots from the costers at Vauxhall Market."

"At that rate, by next Friday, you will be very comfortable," the Lady said with approval.

"You truly mean it, then?" Mr. Dean asked. "You will live here with only the children?"

"Yes." Maggie smiled at him. "But in the meanwhile, I am still at Carrick House. Lady Claire said you were visiting friends? Is his lordship not in need of his lessons this week?"

"Sir Richard and Lady Jermyn have taken Nicholas north to visit Sir Richard's daughter," the Lady said.

"Finding myself with an unexpected holiday on my hands, I boarded the *Flying Dutchman* and here I am." As if to illustrate, Mr. Dean spread his empty hands. "I have friends in Ennismore Gardens, near the Brompton Oratory, who have been most anxious to have me stay. They have no end of amusements and outings planned. I predict I shall be quite exhausted by the time I return."

"How delightful," Lizzie said.

Lucy came out with the tea, only to discover that they did not have cake plates.

"Never mind, dearling," Maggie said with an anxious glance at the Lady, but she did not seem bothered by the lack. "We will simply use our palms for plates, and add china to our shopping list."

"Topping," Lizzie said happily. "I adore looking at china. Royal Morvoren is my favorite."

"Our grandmother's set will have to satisfy you," Maggie told her with a smile. "Though with twenty place settings, we could divide it down the middle and still have plenty for company. I will not tussle with you for the soup tureen. One could bathe a small child in it. I cannot imagine making that much soup for any occasion."

"I am sure Mr. Dean did not come all this way to talk of place settings and soup tureens, girls," the Lady said, laughter bubbling under the words.

"Indeed not—er, I mean, I did have something I wished to discuss with Miss Polgarth." He flushed. "Perhaps when we have finished our tea, you might show me this flock I have heard so much of."

Maggie took her time, for the fire burning in the hearth today was warm and the pleasure of Granny Protheroe's fruit-cake was not to be rushed. As Lizzie and Lucy washed up and the Lady took up Lizzie's pillowcase to work on while she waited, Maggie pulled on her wool coat and tugged her red beret down over her chignon.

42

Mr. Dean offered her his arm and they strolled out to the enclosure.

"I am breeding this particular flock for temperament," she said as he gazed upon the results of her work the previous summer. "The cock has never attacked me, and the hens remained relatively calm for the journey here, so I have some confidence that my theories will bear fruit."

"I am filled with admiration that you can tell a cock from a hen," he said. "I certainly cannot."

"The cock is that large bird there, by the ramp. He can be recognized by his size, as well as his large comb and wattle. You will also observe the spurs on his legs, and his general air of watchfulness."

"Ah. I see I shall have to leave aside my natural delicacy about discussing breeding with a young lady. One does not, you know. Discuss such things."

"One does, here, by necessity," she said with a laugh. "And one presents papers to the London Biological Society discussing it at quite some length. At least, that is my goal for my fourth year. Students are not permitted to present before then."

"Good heavens," he said. "And your guardian? What are Lady Claire's feelings on the matter?"

"She and Doctor Malvern will sponsor me," Maggie said, surprised that she had to point out the obvious. "From here you can see the Carrick Airfield. Have you been there, sir?"

"We passed it on the way. I understand it is one of Lady Claire's many investments."

"Yes. My guardian is a remarkable woman."

"She is not the only one," he said, clearly meaning to

convey a compliment. "Miss Polgarth, I wonder if I might ask you something."

"Certainly." She gazed down the slope to the cheering sight of the airships moored on the field. There was *Athena*, her travel-worn fuselage a deceivingly nondescript buff color. There were several touring balloons with stripes and flags, and a number of sleeker long-distance craft owned by members of Parliament and some of the wealthier families who did not want to keep their ships at Hampstead Heath with the commercial vessels.

And oh, goodness! There was the silver and blue hull of *Swan*! Alice and Sir Ian must have just returned from Edinburgh! She must tell the Lady at once.

Maggie turned, and felt a moment of shock when she realized she had completely forgotten Mr. Dean standing there.

"Mr. Dean, I must—"

"I know we have only been acquainted a short time," he said, apparently not noticing her excitement, "but I must seize my opportunities where I find them. My friends the Northams in Ennismore Gardens are having a few people in this evening for dinner and dancing. I know it is short notice, but I would very much like it if you would accompany me."

Alice and Ian had come to visit! Did Jake know? Maggie began to walk up the grassy slope.

"Miss Polgarth?" He jogged to catch up with her. "Have I offended in being so precipitate?"

"Precip— No, indeed." She must remember her manners, or Grandfather would hear of it, and she could not bear to disappoint him even at a distance.

"Then you will accept my invitation?"

To what? Oh, dinner. "Yes, if that would please you."

"It would. Very much." His smile made his face almost handsome. "I shall call for you at six o'clock, if that is suitable?"

"At Carrick House." Dear me, they would have to leave soon. The chickens were all inside their house. She pulled the lever, and the door ratcheted down, keeping them safe from foxes for the night. She set the locks and turned her attention back to her guest. "Thank you, Mr. Dean."

In the excitement of telling the Lady the news of *Swan's* arrival, and bundling everyone into the landau for a stop at the airfield before they went home, Maggie quite forgot that she had meant to attend a lecture on the flora and fauna of the Thames Valley that evening.

CHAPTER 5

*J*ake fidgeted upon the uncomfortable chair in the lecture hall. Next to him, a large woman gazed raptly at the speaker as he launched into his talk about the plants and animals to be found in the river valley, and how they were adapting their behavior to the increasing encroachment of man, his machines, and his buildings.

Jake was not sure what in the handbill had interested Maggie, but when she had mentioned it the other day, he had been determined to meet her here so she would not have to walk home alone afterward.

And now she had not come.

Half an hour in, he was becoming interested in spite of himself, for the speaker had a fair grasp of land forms and the tendencies man had to use them, several proofs of which theory Jake had already observed from the air.

But still Maggie did not come.

Perhaps he had the date wrong. Jake borrowed a bit of paper from the stout lady and jotted down a few notes that he thought Maggie might find useful. He left the lecture feeling disappointed and cross. At least it had not been a total loss. As the Lady would say, any opportunity to tuck away a useful fact was never a waste of time.

Back at Carrick House, he left the notes under door of the bedroom Maggie and Lizzie shared, and went down to the parlor, from which a racket of conversation was flowing.

"Jake!" Alice, Lady Hollys, leaped up from the sofa she was sharing with the Lady, and flew across the room to hug him.

"When did you land?" he asked, slightly breathless from the impact, and crossed the room for a hearty handshake with Sir Ian. "I was not expecting you for a few days yet. Did you cancel the Irish part of the voyage?"

"We were not expecting to be here, either, and yes, we did," Alice said, tucking herself into the sofa again. "You see …"

She blushed, and her husband said, "You see, we think an addition to our family might be on the horizon, so we returned before the weather became worse."

"An addition!" Jake seized Ian's hand and pumped it. "Congratulations, Captain. That is wonderful news."

"Isn't it?" Sir Ian beamed upon his wife, and she beamed back, and something seemed to twist and break inside Jake.

Why must everyone find happiness but he?

In all fairness, Lewis and Snouts had not found that kind of happiness either, but this did not appear to bother them. Something about the warmth of the connection between Alice and her husband had opened a wound inside him—a wound, he supposed, that had always been there, but had simply scabbed over.

He and Snouts had only hazy memories of their mother, and none at all of their separate fathers. He suspected that she had been a doxy working the saloons of Campbelltown, but he did not really know. He had no experience of love except for what he had found right here. If anyone were to observe a model of conjugal love, he had only to look at the Lady and Dr. Malvern. From the Lady, he had also learned what the love of a mother might look like. And of course he had spent five or six years with Alice, learning what it was to respect and love a woman in the way a student loved and respected his mentor and captain.

But this—this new feeling that seemed to be growing in his breast for Maggie ... well, he had no models for that. No previous experience. And certainly no course to set on a voyage to discover whether she felt the same way.

All this flashed through Jake's mind and heart in the few moments it took Alice and Ian to smile at one another, and for the captain to take Alice's hand.

"So we have come to London so that a doctor may attend upon my wife, and reassure her anxious husband that all is well."

"I might suggest the doctor who attended my mother recently," the Lady said. "She seemed very satisfied with him."

"Thanks, Claire," Alice said gratefully. "I did not know where to start. This is far off my usual course."

"You will be here a day or two, then," Andrew said. "Please come to dinner tomorrow, after your appointment."

"Thank you, that is very kind," Sir Ian said. "We would be delighted."

"Oh, I do wish Maggie had been able to stay this evening," the Lady said. "How she would have loved hearing your news at first hand!"

"Maggie is out?" Jake blurted. He had thought she was upstairs resting after her labors at the cottage.

"Yes, Mr. Dean invited her to dinner and a dance at the home of his friends," Lizzie said. "I don't expect she'll be home for ages."

If Sir Ian had swung a haymaker and caught Jake in the stomach, he could not have felt more stunned. "Mr. Dean?" he croaked.

"Yes, you know—"

"I know who he is." And Jake blundered out of the parlor, blind with hurt and rage, and up the stairs to his own room.

He fell upon the bed like a tree that has succumbed to the axe, and lay there in the dark while a wave of pain took him under. He barely heard the sound of a soft knock.

The door cracked open, letting in a bar of light. "Jake?" Alice whispered. "Are you all right, Navigator?"

"Aye, Captain," he said after a moment. He scrubbed at his face and rolled to a more respectful sitting position.

She pinched the electrics on and sank down beside him on the bed. "What's wrong?"

"Nothing." He cleared his throat. "Captain." She bumped his shoulder with hers, and he could have wept. "It's good to have you home again, Alice. Especially with your good news."

"It's good to be home with the flock. Ian and I make our home wherever we are together, but there's nothing quite like being here at Carrick House. And at Hollys Park. He is anxious to reach the old place, and get it ready for—" Her throat closed. "For the baby."

Jake gave her a keen look, thankful to think of something else besides his own abyss of despair. "Everything is all right, aye?"

"Oh yes. At least, I think so. I feel well. It's just—" She gave a breath of a chuckle. "The thought of me as a mother is … laughable."

"Not half as laughable as the thought of me as a—" Now it was his turn to choke himself off.

"As a what, Jake?" Her blue gaze didn't miss a thing. "Does it have something to do with Maggie's going to dinner with the viscount's tutor?"

He scrubbed his face with his hands and didn't answer.

"We barely got a glimpse of her before she left," Alice said in a conversational tone. "Hardly more than a hug and a kiss. She came down in a tawny silk dinner dress with a flounce of lace about the neckline I could swear was from Venice, and he had brought a nosegay of flowers in a silver holder for her to wear at her belt. She had her hair done up—"

"Stop, Alice," Jake groaned. "You're killing me." For that was her best dress, and she would not have worn it, nor accepted the gift of flowers, if she did not like Mr. Alden Dean more than Jake had realized.

Obligingly, Alice stopped. And waited.

As the silence grew, it dawned on Jake that his captain would not leave the room until he said something. And he would not do so, not for the world.

They were going to be in here a long time.

"How long have you loved her?" she asked softly.

He groaned as she hit the nail on the head and split him open. "My whole life, it seems."

"I don't mean as a sister."

"Neither do I. But it's no good, Alice. She doesn't see me that way. And she doesn't need the likes of me anyhow. She deserves someone fine, and educated, and a gentleman. Like Alden bloody Dean. He's perfect for her." *Perfect* came out from between his teeth, as though he'd chewed up the word and spat it on the floor.

"I don't know about that." Thoughtfully, Alice leaned back on her hands. On the left was a plain gold band, nestled next to the Hollys sapphire.

Another reminder that Jake Fletcher McTavish had nothing to his name to give Maggie but the holly sapling he had not yet planted. Oh, he had his salary from the Corps, and his half interest in *Swan*, and one or two clever investments were piling up thanks to Lewis and the Zeppelin Airship Works, but Maggie had more in the bank than he did. And now she was a woman of property and education, to boot.

What was he?

Moping in his room like a child, that's what. A room that wasn't even his own.

Alice wasn't finished with him. "This Mr. Dean might look good at first glance, but tell me this. Did Maggie give *him* her half of *Swan* after our adventure in Venice?"

"He was probably at bloody Oxford at the time, getting a proper education."

"Was he in Resolution risking his neck for his friends?"

"I wasn't either," Jake said bitterly. "I betrayed my friends on that occasion, if you'll remember."

"Oh, that's right." Alice didn't seem much bothered by bringing up the worst few days of Jake's life. Then again, her stepfather Ned Mose hadn't pushed *her* off his ship at three hundred feet. "But who realized he'd done wrong, and came back to do the right thing?"

"There wasn't much choice. The alternative was to die out there."

"Many a man has had the same choice, and made the

second one to salve his pride," she said firmly. "My dear, you have qualities that are the equal of Maggie's. Don't sell yourself short. Don't be like me," she said softly, sitting up and folding her hands so that her rings were uppermost. "Don't think that everyone else on earth is better than you, when the truth is, Maggie doesn't need everyone else. She needs a man who will love her and stand by her no matter what. As Ian does for me. As Andrew does for Claire. And as John does for Davina." She gave him a sidelong look. "Are you seeing a pattern here, Navigator?"

He surprised himself by smiling. Usually he was better than this at seeing patterns. "Aye, Captain."

"If you love that girl, show her. All the fine, educated words in the dictionary are no good if a man's actions don't match them. And I for one know that you are highly skilled in the action department."

"Aye, Captain. Are you quite finished with your orders for this evening, Captain?"

She rose and dusted off her skirts. "I am. Don't forget them." With a nod, she took her leave.

"I won't," he said softly, but she had already gone.

MAGGIE WAS no stranger to dinners, or to balls either. Why, she had attended the Lady's wedding celebration at Hatley House and been presented to the Queen. But even that occasion, with all its grandeur, had not made her so uncomfortable as this one.

Mr. Dean's friends were kind and welcoming, and the rest of the party unobjectionable. It was clear they were Bloods, but that did not bother her. However, after the third or fourth hint and some gentle teasing during dinner, it became clear to Maggie that his friends considered her to be the object of his affections, and would not take her persistent turning of the subject seriously. It was a relief to leave the room. When she rejoined the ladies in the drawing room, she had the distinct feeling they had been waiting for her.

"Miss Polgarth, do you play?" her hostess Mrs. Northam asked, indicating the piano.

"I am afraid not," she said.

"Oh, such a shame. For Alden is positively transported by music. He is such a rewarding escort at a concert—he knows just when to warn one that the kettledrums are about to join in so one does not jump out of one's seat." She laughed. "I shall be sure to ask him to invite you when next we make up a party."

"I may not have much time for concerts and parties," Maggie said. "I begin my course of study at the University of London next week."

"Indeed," one of the other young ladies said with interest. "A friend is in her first year of the Economics of the Home. She says there are twenty young ladies in her class. Are you one of them?"

"Oh, no," Maggie said. "I was halfway through my second year studying genetics at the University of Bavaria in Munich. I have transferred here in order to conduct my own experiments closer to home, and will take a degree in Applied Biology."

Silence greeted this modest announcement.

"I see we have a budding Wit among us," someone said *sotto voce*.

"Biology?" her hostess said faintly, attempting to smile. "Dear me. How risqué."

The others tittered, as though there were something not quite proper about it. Well, if that was what they wanted ...

"Mr. Dean is recovered, I trust, from our discussion about breeding poultry?" Maggie inquired with false solicitude. "For that is what I am doing. I am selectively breeding one of my flocks for temperament, one for color and feathering, and the third for conformity to the English Poultry Standard."

"Good heavens." Fanning herself, Mrs. Northam walked rapidly to the door, where the gentlemen were coming in. "Kindly do not say such things in mixed company, Miss Polgarth. You will quite put us to the blush."

At least she had made them cease interrogating her.

Dancing was, as always, a pleasure. She had two waltzes with Mr. Dean, and when he asked for a third, she declined. The other gentlemen were pleasant but dull, and she was not sorry when Alden indicated he would take her home.

"I hope you liked my friends," he said in the carriage. "They seemed to like you very much. Though I had no doubt they would."

It had been a long time since she had been driven in a carriage, with horses and a coachman. It was quite the novelty. She observed the coachman's control of the animals with interest. Might horses be bred for temperament also?

"They were very nice," she said absently. Talk of her flock had made her quite anxious about them. She had seen foxes on the hill that morning, and it would not hurt to make certain that the poultry house was secure, since no one was as yet living on the property. "Mr. Dean, would you mind very much if we stopped at my cottage? I wish to check on my birds."

"Vauxhall Gardens is quite a distance out of our way, Miss Polgarth."

She sat back on the cushions, rather hard. "Very well. I will take Lady Claire's steam landau."

"I beg your pardon? You know how to pilot such a thing? Think of the hour!"

"It is barely eleven, sir, and I am worried about foxes."

"I am worried about the propriety of such an escapade. To say nothing of your safety."

Maggie was beginning to lose her patience, and they were coming up on the turn to the bridge. "Then kindly take me to the cottage, as I asked."

"My word, I had not suspected such a gentle young lady of a will as strong as this." He leaned forward. "Vauxhall Gardens, please, Coachman. The young lady will direct you."

"Very good, sir."

They made the turn on to the bridge and Maggie relaxed. "You needn't worry about the time," she assured him. "I only need a minute or two to be certain the birds are in no danger."

"You are very solicitous, Miss Polgarth. I marvel that such creatures as chickens can engender such care."

"Certainly they do," she replied crisply. "Aside from their intelligence and companionship, which make them worthy of any thinking person's solicitude, they represent months of labor and study. My grandfather and I have quite an investment in them."

"Ah, I had not forgotten that your grandfather is Polgarth the poultryman," he said. "How you have risen in the world!

My hat is off to you." And he tipped it in her direction with a smile.

"Risen, sir?" Had someone told him of her years as a street sparrow?

"That is the benefit of living in the metropolis, I suppose," he said as the carriage passed the airfield. "One may use one's talents to leave the farmyard behind for ever."

If she had felt impatient with him before, it was nothing to the dangerous simmering of her temper now. "Might I remind you, sir, that my grandfather's knowledge of breeding and genetics has produced a flock known throughout Cornwall for its quality. His expertise is not questioned even as far away as Bristol and here in London. His influence extends much farther than—as you imply—the *farmyard*." She took a breath to calm herself. "Coachman, the right turn here, if you please. The gate is on the right in fifty yards."

Mr. Dean turned to her as the carriage slowed. "I meant no offense. Polgarth is a capital old man, and as you say, he knows his chickens. I only meant—"

"Is this the gate, miss?" the coachman asked.

"Yes, it is, thank you." When he pulled the horses to a stop, Maggie climbed to the ground with agility, despite her silk skirts, and without benefit of assistance. "Mr. Dean, no need to get down. I will only be a moment."

"I cannot let you wander about alone in the dark." He climbed down, too, but she was already opening the gate.

"I beg you, do not trouble yoursel—"

A figure rose out of the darkness on the other side of the stone wall, and Maggie shrieked as her heart nearly stopped in her chest.

CHAPTER 6

*C*alling himself all kinds of a fool for not being able to go to sleep while Maggie was out in the company of Alden Dean, Jake had finally given it up altogether. He had risen, dressed, collected a shovel and the holly tree from where it languished in the garden, and borrowed Lewis's two-seater steam landau for the trip over to Maggie's cottage.

In rambling about the place, moonglobe held high, trying to decide where to plant the sapling, he checked the chickens' house and found it secure, though a shadow slipped away out of sight as he approached.

"Not on my watch, you rascal," he told it, testing door and windows and finding them in order. Because of the birds' value, the doors of all the houses bore a series of interlocking cylinders and turning latches that were opened not with a key, but with a sequence of pressure studs. Maggie had the idea from the pirates' door under the cellar at Seacombe House. These locks came as close to guaranteeing the hens' safety from two-legged foxes as anything could.

In all, the front gate was the best place for a tree, he

decided. If holly meant protection, then it was either that or the front door, but as it grew, it might block the light from the window, and that would never do.

The gate it was.

He had just finished tamping down the soil around the little tree when he heard the clip-clop of hooves coming down the road. Only the very poor or the very rich rode in horse-drawn vehicles, and if it were a wagon full of miscreants from the south bank …

Jake pocketed his moonglobe, stepped into the darkness next to the stone wall, and hefted the shovel in both hands.

The next thing he heard was—of all things—Maggie's voice. Seconds later she opened the gate, and in his surprise, he stepped out into the light of the carriage lamps.

She shrieked—and rammed her hand down the side of her silk skirt. Where a pocket should be—and was not, in her evening gown. Where her lightning pistol should be—and was not, in her moment of need.

"Maggie! It's all right. It's only me."

Her empty hand went to her heart over her short, fur-trimmed evening jacket. "Jake?"

"I say, what is this?" Alden Dean burst through the gate and pushed Maggie behind him with one arm.

She stumbled in the hard soil Jake had dug up, and in his outrage that Dean should have manhandled her that way, Jake nearly swung the shovel. But she regained her footing with the help of the nearest upright object.

"Ouch! What on earth—?" She had inadvertently grasped the stout little holly sapling, which had done its best to protect itself, right through her glove. "Where did this come from?"

"I just planted it," Jake said lamely.

"Explain yourself, sir," Alden Dean demanded, quite as though he had a right to.

"I brought it from Gwynn Place," he said to Maggie. "As a housewarming present."

Now both gloved hands pressed themselves to her heart. His planting it at nearly midnight did not seem to her at all unusual. "For me? Oh Jake, how very kind you are." She turned to regard the little tree with delight. "I venture to say it is from Grandfather's garden."

"There you would be right. I could not sleep, so I commandeered Lewis's landau, and here we are."

"Thank you!" She flung her arms around him in a hug.

Jake had a single moment to feel her slender solidity between his own two paws—one of which still held the shovel —to take one breath of her scent—lavender—to feel the soft press of her cheek.

She broke away. "I came to check the chicken houses." Her voice was a little muffled.

"No fear, I already have. A fox slunk away as I approached, but all is secure. He had no way in. Alfred and I made certain the houses were solid."

"There, Miss Polgarth," Alden Dean said, as though this had been a point of argument.

Jake had forgotten the man. At this rate, the holly tree would do more to protect Maggie than Jake would, standing there like a numpty with the scent of lavender in his nostrils.

"There was no need to come all this way," Dean went on. Chiding her. "Your brother had everything in hand. Though I shall not remark upon the peculiarity of gardening at such an hour on a January night."

"Mr. McTavish is not my brother," Maggie said flatly, ignoring the rest of his nonsense.

"Oh, of course. One forgets, your house being full of young men who were Lady Claire's wards."

"What are you getting at, Mr. Dean?" Jake said suspiciously. He did not care for the man's tone.

"Why, nothing at all. The point is, Miss Polgarth, that it is high time that I saw you back to Carrick House."

"Jake may take me in the landau," she said. "After all, we are going to the same house." Now her tone held a silky challenge. It was clear the man's veiled criticism of the Lady's household arrangements had not merely been Jake's imagination.

"Certainly not," Mr. Dean huffed. "A gentleman ends the evening by returning the lady to her home. I should not dream of allowing convenience to supersede propriety."

"Even if I should request it?"

"Even then."

"I rather dislike it when notions of propriety supersede my wishes, Mr. Dean."

"I rather think you might need more practice in that regard, Miss Polgarth." He sounded jocular, as though he thought himself to be engaging in witty banter.

Jake's hands tightened on the shovel. The idiot would be patting her on the head next—she, who had saved England from invasion by the pretender to the French throne!

"Then it should come as no—" Maggie stopped. Her head lifted—turned—the way it used to do when she and Lizzie scouted, and she strained to hear what her sister's sharper ears had already detected.

And now Jake heard it, too. Footsteps on the road. A

number of feet. Six pairs at least. There was no drunken singing, no orderly step of the constables on night watch.

"Maggie, go into the house," Jake said.

"But the hens—"

"The hens are safe. We made the windows smaller than a sweep's boy could get into, and nothing is getting past those locks."

"Are you armed?"

He cursed himself for a fool. "No. You?"

"This wretched dress."

"Into the house, then, quickly."

"Sir!" called the coachman from the road. "I don't like the look of this. Several men are approaching."

Mr. Dean found his voice. "What is going on?"

Jake swallowed his impatience and silently wished him to Hades. "Tell him to go. Get in the house."

"Go? But how will I—"

"You may go, Coachman," Maggie called. "My brother is here, and he will see us home in the landau."

"Will you be all right, miss?"

"Quite all right. Please find a constable and send him along, though, if you would."

"Right-o, miss."

"Wait!" Alden Dean tried to stop the carriage, but it was already too late.

It bowled off smartly, leaving one less person in harm's way. Maggie yanked Mr. Dean nearly off his feet, so that he stumbled after her. The key lay under a slate forming one of the steps. She unlocked the door and pushed him inside.

"What are you doing?"

"Hush. With any luck, they will not have heard us, and will pass us by."

"Who?"

"The men from a south bank gang approaching along the road. Didn't you hear what the coachman said?"

"No," he snapped. "I was busy wondering why you asked Jake if he was armed."

"Because—obviously—a pistol would be useful if the cottage is their object." It was too risky to activate the electricks. She shook a moonglobe into life and cast about for anything she could use as a weapon.

The iron frying pan. That would do.

Jake had a shovel. What else?

"But why should— Miss Polgarth, I am all at sea. You behave as though you expect to be attacked."

"I do."

"But surely no one would dare accost us! I, at least, am a gentleman!"

She glanced at him with a frown. "Have you even been on the south bank, Mr. Dean?"

"Why, no, except to attend a play at the old Vauxhall Gardens, when I was a child."

"Things have changed since then." She said no more, only took down her mother's portrait and ran upstairs with it. She slid it under the pieces of the beautiful wrought-iron bedstead that had been delivered day before yesterday and which she had not yet had time to set up.

Wrought iron.

The whorls, spirals, and flower-like pieces were meant to be hooked together to form the head- and footboards. But for now, might some of them be large enough to be used as weapons?

"Wish us luck, Mama," she whispered to the portrait, and ran down the stairs with her hands full.

Mr. Dean gaped at her. "What is all that?"

"Bits of my bed," she said shortly. "Here. Can you swing this at a man if you have to?"

He stared at the iron whorl in her hand, big enough to hang a pork roast from, and looking rather like a hook at that. "Swing— Are you saying it will come to fisticuffs?"

For heaven's sake, for a man with an Oxford education, he took forever to apprehend a point. "I hope so. If they are carrying firearms, however, these will not do much to help our situation." She handed it to him and hefted a similar one for herself. The good thing about this was that if it got bent over someone's skull, repairing it was simply a matter of taking it to the blacksmith.

"Good heavens. How appalling."

"Give it a swing," she suggested. "Test its weight."

"I certainly shall not." He laid it on the mantel rather as though it might turn into a glossy black snake at any moment.

There came a shout from outside and then the clang of a shovel against stone.

Someone screamed.

"We know you, Jake McTavish!" a second man shouted. "Tell your thrice-damned Lady that Jem Spivey runs the south bank now, and 'e'll 'ave 'er property, ta ever so."

"This ent the Lady's property, Jem Spivey," Maggie heard Jake say. "It belongs to a poulterer."

"Ent wot we 'eard. Off you go. It's ours now."

Maggie snatched up the hook from the mantel so that she held one in each hand. "Mr. Dean, make yourself useful. Send a tube to Carrick Airfield immediately. Tell them we need help."

"But why would—"

"Just do it!"

He scurried into the kitchen, and in a moment she heard the whoosh of a tube being sucked into the pneumatic postal system.

"Bring out the frying pan," she ordered over her shoulder. "It's on the stove. Perhaps you'll be more comfortable swinging that." It was less likely he would miss, too.

"Your last chance, Jem Spivey," Jake said, closer now to the house.

His answer was a chorus of yells and pounding feet, and seconds later Jake leaped through the door and slammed it. Fists pounded, and he barely got the latch down before a shoulder hit the sturdy planks.

Maggie wound the mechanism on the articulated side-board. It flipped and tipped and reconstructed itself in half a dozen configurations across the dining room floor, and fetched up against the front door. Jake leaped out of the way and it built itself into a door shape, its heavy weight presenting a second barrier.

Two men were flinging themselves shoulder first against the door, but it would not budge.

"Well done, sideboard," Jake told it with some admiration.

Before Maggie could take a breath, the parlor window exploded inward and a rock from the garden landed on her lovely old sofa. Her evening slippers crunched on the glazing as she leaped forward and brought down the flats of both iron hooks on the head and shoulders of the man wriggling through.

With a shriek, he fell backward into the garden. In his stead, the barrel of a gun was rammed into the jagged aperture.

Without a word, Jake dropped his shovel, grabbed the barrel with both hands, and yanked it out of its owner's grasp. He flipped it and discharged it out of the window in one smooth motion.

Deafened, Maggie could still scream like a banshee with triumph, the shrill sound combining eerily with the scream of the dying man outside.

"Reg! Reg!" someone wept. Then, "I'll 'ave your guts for garters!"

The dining-room window blew inward, a brick landed on the dining table in a shower of glass, and a second gun barrel poked through.

A double blast discharged into the wall where the sideboard had been, knocking chunks of plaster to the floor. Before the enemy could remove the gun and reload it, Alden Dean raced in from the kitchen, leaped through the smoke, and swung the cast-iron frying pan with all his strength. *Clang!* The window sill acted as a fulcrum, and the hot gun barrel bent with the force of the blow. It clattered to the floor, now useless as anything but a club.

Mr. Dean grinned like a death's head in delight. "By George, that showed them!"

"Don't count your chickens," Jake said grimly, his shoulders to the wall as he peered around the jagged window frame. Frigid air poured into the room. "There are still four left."

"Have we got all the guns?" Maggie asked, breathing hard, her hands flexing on the iron hooks.

"Looks like."

"Jake, take the shovel. Alden, your pan. Come with me."

With a jerk of her chin, she indicated they should follow her out the kitchen door. They circled the house to see Jem Spivey and his three remaining mates in heated argument in front of the door.

With a blood-curdling yell, Maggie ran at them. One broke and fled, running into the holly tree at the gate and bouncing off it with a cry of pain before he took off down the road. The remaining three ranged themselves in a line, bending their knees to meet the onslaught, their hands fisted in fighting position.

One of them straightened in surprise at the sight of a young lady in a silk evening gown—Maggie swung her iron hook with all her might—it caught him on the side of the head. As he crashed to the ground like a fallen tree, she whirled and swung with the other. But her feet tangled in her skirts and she tripped over the first man.

With a yell, Jem Spivey fell on her, screaming invective— tearing at her skirts—yanking at her bodice. She rammed the second hook up between them for a wedge as the weight of his body drove all the breath from her lungs and the foul gush of his breath choked her.

Of all the times she had come close to it or even imagined it in the dark of night, this was *not* how Marguerite Polgarth had meant to die.

She could not breathe. Jem Spivey was the size of an ox, and crushing the life out of her.

Jake ...

Jake ...

The darkness swarmed in and she went under.

CHAPTER 7

*J*ake swung the shovel at the remaining man while Alden Dean took a roundhouse blow with the frying pan. The force of both meeting on either side of his skull toppled the last miscreant, where he lay unmoving.

"Maggie!" Jake pounded over to the scene of destruction near the door. "Maggie!"

"Dear heaven, the blood!" cried Dean, and flung himself to his knees beside what they could see of her slender form.

Jake's heart had been drubbing like a steam engine, but at the sight of her in the moonlight, it seemed to stop altogether. He and Dean shoved the huge carcass off her and a terrible sound was torn from his throat as Jake saw the sheet of glistening blood.

Blood everywhere. On the ground. On the body. But mostly on Maggie. Her jacket and bodice had been torn nearly off, the silk soaked and dull with it. Her face—her hair—her hands, limp and white and stained with it.

"Maggie." Hot tears cascaded down Jake's cheeks—the only

warmth it seemed his body possessed. He slid his bleeding, cold paws under her and lifted her with infinite gentleness. "Oh, Maggie, my dear little love."

"Where is she injured?" Dean rasped. "We must stop the bleeding if we can."

But how to tell the source when there was so much of it? With one hand, Jake fished the moonglobe out of his pocket and held it close to her. Her throat—her chest—a head wound —where? Where was the source of the blood? And was it already too late?

Maggie gasped and opened her eyes.

Jake's whole being leaped, though he did not move for fear of injuring her further. "Maggie? Where is your wound, dear? Where does it hurt?"

"Can't—breathe—"

A punctured lung? She was done for. The blood seemed to drain out of Jake's head.

"We must get her to a doctor, quickly." Dean pulled away the remains of the elegant bodice and dropped the sopping mass in the gravel.

"I don't need—a doctor," Maggie gasped, trying feebly to cover her lacy chemise. "Only—air."

"But you—the blood!" Jake croaked. "Do not move. You will hurt yourself."

"Jem—Spivey."

Jake did not spare the body a glance. "He'll come round, I suppose. But we must get—"

"The—blood is his."

"What?" Alden Dean ceased his attempts to find a wound, and Maggie batted his hands away.

"Stop. I am not hurt. The blood is Spivey's."

Still dragging in great breaths of air, she felt around on the ground and pulled a wrought-iron hook from under her skirts. "This."

With a cry that could have been discovery or horror, Alden Dean leaped to his feet and rolled Spivey's body over. Sure enough, a jagged rent in his throat still trickled with blood.

"She got an artery," Dean said with wonder.

"I did not mean to." Maggie seemed in no hurry to stand, so Jake felt no compunction about pulling her into his lap and holding her closer. She wore only her chemise and corset, and after such a shock, he must keep her warm.

He felt around until his hand closed on her jacket. Blood-stained though it was, it had fared better than her bodice. "Put this on. Your dress is beyond help."

Obediently, she did, pulling the warm woollen lining close about her. "He fell on me, frothing with rage. All I could do was wedge the iron between us. I did not think—" Tears pooled in her eyes.

Tears that Jem Spivey did not deserve. But now another thought had finally penetrated the haze of fear and relief in Jake's mind. "Maggie—you know what must be done."

A tear trickled down her cheek. "We must bury them? Or ought we to wait for the night watch?"

"No. You've killed the leader of the south bank gang. You must claim what is his. Now, before that boy who got away gets back to the squat. Before they realize what has happened and elect one of Spivey's lieutenants." He glanced at the bodies in the garden. "His remaining lieutenants."

"Oh, no," Maggie whispered, and turned her face into Jake's coat as though seeking protection. "I cannot."

"You must, dearling, or they will never stop coming."

"But I am not like the Lady! I don't want to be the leader of the south bank gang. I want to go to university and raise my flock and live in my house with y—" She stopped with a choked sound. "I can't."

With y—? Years of happiness? Young children? *You?*

Jake did not dare speculate. He could not afford to hope. Not when a job had to be done and her safety was at stake.

"You must," he said again, for in truth there was no way around it. "Come. I know where their squat is, if they haven't moved in the last year. We'll take Lewis's landau."

In the chill air, the distinctive sound of a landau sounded outside in the road, then a pounding of feet. The bottom fell out of his stomach. Too late. Here came the gang. Another contingent must have been waiting in case something went wrong, tipped off by that boy. He would have done the same had he been Spivey.

"Maggie!" he said, getting to his feet and pulling her up. "They're coming."

"Jake!" called a frantic but familiar voice from the darkness outside the gate. "Maggie, are you all right?"

"Alice!" Maggie sagged against Jake's body in relief, then caught herself and straightened.

She stepped away, pulling the jacket tightly about her as Alice, Sir Ian, Benny Stringfellow, and two of the watchmen from the airfield tumbled through the gate. All three of the crew of *Swan* carried lightning pistols in each hand, their glass globes already flickering with tendrils of blue light. They had been sleeping on *Swan*, and clearly the watch had called there first for reinforcements before coming to their aid.

"What in heaven's name…?" Alice gaped at the bodies in the garden. "Are we too late? Are you hurt?"

"Too late for them," Mr. Dean said. "Good evening, Lady Hollys. Sir Ian."

"Bloody smoking he—" Benny stopped to gawk at her bloodstained silk skirts. "Maggie, wot's 'appened to you?"

"I killed Jem Spivey," Maggie said with admirable brevity. "Accidentally. But regardless, I must confront his gang and claim his possessions and position, or there will never be an end to it."

"Ah." Benny nodded, his face full of sympathy. "I don't envy you that."

"What on earth does this mean?" Mr. Dean demanded.

"Maggie, I don't understand, either," Alice said. "You're covered in blood. We must get you home to Claire immediately."

"Benny will explain," Maggie said, a note of weary hopelessness in her voice that broke Jake's heart.

This was not the life she wanted. Not the future any civilized person wanted if they had a choice. He knew that. But he also knew that if Maggie did not do what was expected, as the Lady had been forced to years ago, she likely would not have a future. For the gangs did not respect weakness, only strength and cleverness.

"We'll need the loan of your pistols, Alice," Jake said when Benny had finished putting them in the picture. "No sense going into this unarmed."

"No sense going into this at all," she retorted. "But we're still coming with you."

"Ask Lady Claire," Maggie said. "Six years ago she was in this position, and it changed her life."

"All of our lives," Jake added.

"And here I thought I knew all there was to know of her,"

Alice said in wondering tones. But she handed over one of her pistols to Maggie. After a moment, her husband handed one of his to Jake.

"No argument," Ian said. "You'll need backup and we're all you've got."

Jake pocketed the pistol, now humming happily. Maggie's fingers curled around the grip. In her other hand she held the iron hook.

"No argument here," Jake confessed. "It will be like old times. We can use some help getting the bodies into Lewis's landau. I think there is a canvas tarpaulin in the garden shed. He'll never forgive me if I allow his leather seats to be stained with miscreant blood."

MAGGIE SHIVERED in the rush of the midnight air, the sorry state of her evening jacket making it less useful than it could have been, as Jake piloted the landau deep into the warrens of the south bank. Perhaps her shivers were more shock than temperature. Perhaps they were fear of the confrontation to come. Or, more likely they were both those things, with a dollop of terror that her friends had been dragged into this.

People she cared about.

Loved.

For as the oxygen had returned to her lungs and her head had cleared, she had heard Jake say the words she had been wishing for half her life. Had never confessed to anyone she wanted to hear, not even Lizzie. Had thought she would never hear.

Maggie, my dear little love.

Had it really been true? Or had she hallucinated them in her extremity, believing she was going to suffocate to death?

Regardless, she had blurted out her most secret dream to him, or nearly, catching herself just in time in case it *had* been all in her head. For no matter how she had come to feel for him since she had left her girlhood behind, he was still as close to a brother as a man could be. He had never shown her more affection than a brother would, and his thoughtful acts of the last few weeks—even the holly tree—were no more than those of a considerate sibling.

No, she could not take those words at more than their face value. He obviously loved her as a sister, and she was a fool for reading any more into them.

But she must not think of them now. For they were slowing to a stop in the middle of a silent square in a tumbledown stew, the airfield's jalopy jammed with their friends slowing behind them. A moment of observation revealed to Maggie's heightened, experienced senses that while the tiny square might be silent, it was the silence of watchfulness. The motionless second just before the cat sprang.

Jake got out of the pilot's seat and, with Sir Ian's help, dragged the canvas tarpaulin on to the wet, noisome cobbles and unrolled the bodies, laying them out one by one, in a row.

As they did, lights appeared in windows. Shadows in door-ways. Figures in alleys.

Silent. Watching. Tensing.

When all the bodies were arrayed, Jake nodded at Maggie. For they both had seen this done before.

Maggie leapt up on the running board of the landau, humming pistol in one hand and iron hook in the other.

"I know you can see me," she shouted. "I know you know me. I am Maggie, ward of the Lady of Devices."

A man stepped out of a doorway, his hands on his hips, wearing a stained canvas apron like a robe of state. Two others flanked him. Alice, Ian, and the two watchmen fanned out behind the landaus, pistols at the ready.

"Wot business does the ward of the Lady 'ave wiv us?" the man in the apron called. "For we gots no business wiv 'er."

"I say you lie," she called back, brutal as a blunt instrument. "For Jem Spivey tried to take what is mine. I have killed him for his presumption. So I claim his squat, his possessions, and his men, that belonged to the Cudgel before him, and to Lightning Luke Jackson before *him*."

Doors slammed. Windows went up. A thunder of feet sounded on stairs, and in less than a minute, the square had filled with ragged men, horrified women, and filthy children who darted hither and yon to get a better look. For the fact that she knew the antecedents of the gang frightened these people who thought they were invisible. What else did she know? And what would she do to them with that knowledge?

The aproned man approached the bodies with caution, his eyes white-rimmed and riveted on the lightning pistol. "I'll 'ave proof."

"As you like. And then I'll have my claim. What is your name?"

"They call me the Costerman, on account of my stall in Leadenhall." He bent and gestured for a lamp. The light played over the still features of the men on the ground. "Cor," he said on a long breath of disbelief, "she's done for Cray and the Dunlevy brothers, too."

When he stood, his face was waxy, his gaze apprehensive

as it moved from the lightning pistol, with its impatient flickering, to the iron hook gripped in her hand. Then he took in Jake, as though he had only this moment realized he knew him.

"We could do for you right here and now," the Costerman said bravely.

"You could." Maggie raised the iron hook with a hand that did not shake, and pointed the business end at him. "But as I went down, I'd make certain you were the first to fall on this piece of iron that did for Spivey, straight through his neck. Is that what you want? Say the word, and I'll oblige you."

"Nay," he said after a moment's consideration of the hook, as though he were trying to see the blood on it. He swallowed. "We don't want no more death 'ere." He raised his voice. "I yield to the claim of Iron Maggie, killer of Jem Spivey, Joe Cray, and the Dunlevy brothers."

A collective gasp went up from the crowd, and a rustle of agitation as anxious faces turned to the Costerman. As Maggie remembered from her days on the street, sometimes the devil you knew was better than the devil you didn't. Everyone in the square was invested in what happened in the next few minutes.

As for *Iron Maggie*? Well, if it meant she didn't have to die tonight, she would take the sobriquet.

And she would take something else, too.

She would take her life back.

Her gaze locked with that of the Costerman. "I see that you are a man of sense. That you care for the wellbeing of the coves and sparrows in your charge. So I will strike a bargain with you."

"Aye?" he said cautiously. Half his attention still remained on her weapons, the other half on her face, for he could predict her movements if he kept a close watch on her.

"I will cede the leadership of the gang to the Costerman as my first lieutenant, on one condition."

"Cede," he repeated.

"Assign," she said in an undertone.

"Ah. Go on," he said more loudly. "Name your condition, Iron Maggie. If it is not acceptable, you die."

"If it is not acceptable, we both die, and the living will be left to the accounting of Jake Fletcher, whom some of you know." Her voice was so calm a faraway part of her brain wondered how she was managing it.

Some members of the crowd stirred. Clearly, their memories were long and accurate. Jake's slow grin as he cocked the lightning pistol back upon his shoulder would have terrified her had she not known him so well.

"My condition is this," she said clearly, so all could hear. "The Costerman becomes my trusted lieutenant. You will consider him your leader, save only in matters of life and death, when he will consult with me. And in return, I claim all of Vauxhall Gardens, to include my property, that of my neighbors, the Carrick Airfield, the Morton Glass Works, and the Vauxhall Market, as my domain exclusively. You will leave it unmolested, except as I call upon you to aid me in its defense." She raised the hook high in the air. "Do we have an agreement?"

"Aye," said the Costerman.

"Aye!" shouted the crowd. "Aye for Iron Maggie!"

"I seal our agreement in iron and lightning!" she shouted, and fired the lightning pistol up into the air.

The boys screamed with delight as the bolt burned

through the frosty night and detonated upon the deserted stone tower of an abandoned church, dancing along its iron gutters, up its gaping, empty window frames, and at last finding the bell, which glowed blue and chimed in an echo of its former toils until the charge dissipated in its wood supports.

The bolt would never have gone so far had not the charge been stored up so long. Had she actually fired it at the Costerman, he would have been vaporized on the spot.

The crowd cheered at this spectacular entertainment—or perhaps it was a shout of terror at this proof of her lethal potential. They surged forward to take the bodies of their erstwhile leaders, dragging them away on the canvas tarpaulin to goodness only knew what unsavory end.

"Will you take the cash box?" the Costerman said to Maggie, standing his ground in a manner that caused her to respect his bravery.

The Lady's actions in a similar situation flashed through Maggie's memory. "Bring it to me."

In moments, two men brought it out of the squat and set it down before her with a heavy clank. The Costerman opened it with a key and threw back the lid.

"I want the contents distributed evenly to every man, woman and child among you," she said as loudly as before, so that no one should mistake her. "I've no doubt that each has suffered in the getting of it, so each should benefit by the giving of it."

This time the cheer held no terror, and a chain quickly formed as the money was distributed, while little boys darted and dove for fallen pennies.

When the box was empty, Maggie handed her pistol to

Jake, and offered her hand to the Costerman. "I wish you good fortune, a warm fire, and food on your table," she told him.

"I wish you the same," he said. "Farewell. For now."

"You have my support if you need it, you know."

The man nodded, his gaze flicking once again to the lightning pistols. "We're not like to forget it."

With that, Maggie glanced at Jake, who handed her in to Lewis's landau as though she were a queen. Alice and Ian and the others climbed into the jalopy, and the little parade left the square with all the dignity of Queen Victoria leaving Windsor via the Long Walk.

It was not until they reached the ancient ruined stadium of the Kennington Oval that Maggie dropped the iron whorl from her bedstead on the floor by her feet, and sobs of terror and relief overcame her.

CHAPTER 8

From the kitchen doorway, Lady Claire and Alice surveyed the wreckage that had once been Maggie's pristine little home. Lucy's eyes were huge, and Alfred hugged himself about the middle as though to give himself comfort, or protection.

Wordlessly, Claire took Maggie into her arms. "My darling, words cannot express how glad I am that you were not here alone when this happened." She kissed Maggie's hair.

How comforting it was to be held close to the Lady's heart!

Hours before, Maggie and Jake had left Alden Dean to make up a story for his friends about why he had stumbled into their house at four in the morning. They had not had to make up any sort of a tale for the Lady and Andrew, who had met them on the landing in their wrappers and known at once what had happened.

Maggie had spent the next hour in the bath, scrubbing the blood—both real and imagined—off her skin. While he waited his turn, Jake burned her dress and jacket at the bottom of the garden. Then they had both fallen into their beds for some much needed sleep.

"So you are the leader of the south bank now," Claire murmured as she released her. "I must admit I could not have predicted this."

"You should have seen her, Claire," Alice said. "She was like —well, like you when your temper is up and a job has to be done. I daresay she could have taken on that crowd herself."

"Iron Maggie," Lucy breathed. "I shall have to be extra careful not to burn the toast, lest you hook me with a bit of your bed."

Maggie laughed—astonished at herself that she could laugh at all. "The gang will be so disappointed when they find out they were cowed into submission by a piece of a bedstead, won't they?"

"And my lightning pistol," Alice reminded her.

"Yes, it was difficult to argue with that," Maggie agreed. "Perhaps we had best keep the part about the bed a secret."

"And you'll be happy to know that the Lady of Devices still strikes fear into the hearts of men," Alice said to Claire.

"Heavens." Claire only smiled a catlike smile, and said no more.

"Come, let us get to work and set the house to rights," Lucy said. "I don't like to see it this way, not one bit."

"And how are you going to get that cupboard out from in front of the door?" Alice wanted to know. "It must weigh as much as your steam boiler. Come to that, how did you wrestle it over there in the first place?"

"Let us clean up the glass in the dining room and I will show you," Maggie told her.

They got to work with brushes and mops, sweeping up

glass and crushed plaster and scrubbing blood from the floors. Snouts arrived midmorning with an ironmaster and glaziers, to replace the front windows. Alfred repaired the plaster. And when Maggie wound the key and directed the articulated sideboard to return to its place in the dining room, Alice stared openmouthed as it crossed the floor in its higgledy-piggledy fashion and built itself into an orderly oblong once more.

Maggie checked the drawer where the Gwynn Place silver had been. "Well done, sideboard," she told it affectionately. "You have remembered where I put the silver."

"You're talking to the furniture," Alice said, looking at her askance.

"I am," Maggie said. "It seems to like it. And it helped to save our lives last night, so I will say thank you to it, too." She gave it a grateful pat.

Alice merely raised her eyebrows, and said no more.

Jake came down a few minutes later with her mother's portrait. "Your bed is a proper bed now, Maggie, mattress and all. I set up the one in the other room, too. Is that for Lucy?" He re-hung the portrait over the mantel, then tousled the little girl's hair, to no effect whatever, for she had braided it up in a crown like Maggie's.

Lucy nodded, and beamed up at him. "I shall give it up when we have company, of course, and sleep on a cot behind the boiler like Alfred. I have never had a room of my own before."

"Neither have I, in fact," Maggie said on a laugh. "It has always been Lizzie and me, whether squat or manor house."

The cottage was neither, but with her mother's gentle face looking out at them, it was once more her home.

"Who is talking about me?" Lizzie came in the back door, her hair tied up in a kerchief, stripping the gloves from her hands. "I've managed to hide the evidence, Maggie, though I must say you have a bloodthirsty lot of chickens. They were attempting to peck up the stained gravel outside."

"They like the color red, and do eat small bits of gravel," the Lady said. "But I must say if you have managed to clear that great bloodstain away, my hat is off to you. It was utterly gruesome."

"Nothing a bit of cold water, a wire brush, and a spade couldn't fix," Lizzie said briskly. "I say, Maggie, where did that holly tree by the gate come from? It wasn't here before."

Maggie glanced shyly at Jake. "Jake brought it from Grandfather's garden for me."

"I planted it last night, just before all the excitement began," Jake said, reddening as though he had been caught out doing something other than being in the right place at the right time. "If your language of flowers says it means *protection* and *domestic happiness*, then it got the first part right, young as it is. Took a bite out of one of the miscreants on his way out, it did."

"That's it!" Maggie said suddenly. "That is what I will call the cottage. In fact, after this, it could have no other name."

"What, Maggie?" Lucy wanted to know.

"Why, Holly Cottage." Maggie couldn't help giving Jake an enormous smile of gratitude and discovery. Jake looked rather like he'd been poleaxed. "It's perfect."

"And it fits rather better on a sign than some of your other ideas," Lizzie told her. "I'm starving. Did we bring anything to eat?"

～

"I BROUGHT BASKETS OF FOOD—THEY are in the landau," Claire said, laughing. Only Lizzie could go from washing away blood to demanding her tea in less than a minute. "Jake, while everything is being set out, would you escort me down to see how the flock is faring?"

"Aye, Lady," he said. "I'll just put these tools away."

Maggie gave Claire a quizzical look, as if to say, *I should be the one to show you, should I not?* But Claire only smiled reassuringly and said, "We won't be long. I am rather hungry myself."

By which Maggie got the message: *I want a word alone with Jake.*

For the provenance of the holly tree had confirmed the rather astonishing contents of a tube Claire had received from Polgarth the poultryman not long after their return from Gwynn Place.

My dear Lady Claire,

Knowing the modesty of my granddaughter and the taciturn nature of the man Jake Fletcher McTavish, I thought it best to let a hint fall by this means.

The young man took away a sapling from the garden, but not before I winkled out of him that it was to be a gift for our Maggie. To own the truth, I thought he was on my doorstep in the dark of night to ask for our girl's hand. Being a man of plain speech, I told him I would not object, should he ever work up the courage to ask. Perhaps I was forward. Or mistaken. Was I? Anyroad, I know he has your trust, and therefore he has mine.

I hope you and the good doctor keep well. We go on as ever here, but I do miss the sight of both my young ladies, coming through the garden with such joy about them.

My love always,
Gerran Polgarth

Claire had kept its contents to herself, until the events of last night had caused her to realize the more astonishing suppositions in the letter might be the truth after all.

Jake joined her, and offered her his arm. Their footsteps crunched in the sere grass, still tipped with frost in the shady spots. Maggie's chickens, seeing that the sun had reached a certain depth in the sky, judged it prudent to follow their leisurely way back to their house.

"How quickly many hands can set to rights the Spivey gang's destruction," Claire said by way of beginning.

"Aye." For the space of three steps, Jake said no more. Then, "I've never been so thankful in all my life that I could not sleep. What are the odds that she would decide to check on her hens, and that I would be here planting the sapling?"

"I must say that I wish neither of you had been here," Claire admitted. "The gang would have wreaked its destruction on an empty house and gone home, congratulating themselves upon their bravery."

"Aye, but you know as well as I that it would be only a matter of time before they returned. The thing is settled now, and in a manner that still takes my breath away when I think of it."

"Maggie's brush with death has certainly taken mine." Claire's throat tightened at the terrible might-have-beens.

"Lady, oh, that moment when I saw her on the ground—and the blood—"

Jake was not a man given to tears, but his throat closed up and he lost the ability to speak another word. Claire busied herself with the chickens while the rooster escorted his ladies into their house. She set the locks on door and gate, and when she returned to his side, Jake had regained his self-control.

She gazed up at him, this tall, lanky, dangerous young man who had by turns tolerated her, betrayed her, begged her forgiveness, and in the end come to love her. Now, it was clear that she had underestimated his capacity for love, for loyalty, and for sheer bravery in the face of terrible odds when it came to a person even closer to his heart.

"You are in love with our Maggie, aren't you, Jake?" she asked softly.

Jake flinched as though she had struck him, and turned away with a groan. "First Alice, now you. Is it so obvious? Do you think she knows, Lady? I could not bear it if I've given myself away. If I've burdened her with feelings she does not want."

"How could anyone who experienced the events of last night see the demonstration of your feelings as a burden?"

His eyes held agony. "But can she return them? For she is educated—well to do—with a future. A home of her own. A career. And I?" He could hold her gaze no longer. "I am a man with a past I'd rather forget."

"Everyone in our house—save possibly Dr. Malvern— could say the same, Jake. Come. You and Maggie share your past. There is no shame in it. You did the best you could, until you could do better."

"Aye, but neither you nor she betrayed your friends in the worst way possible."

So the memory of Resolution still tormented him, did it?

Well, Claire had had a nightmare born of those memories a time or two herself. "Neither she nor I paid for our betrayals in the way you did, either," she told him gently. "You were reborn out of that lake a different man. You must not let the mistakes of the past affect your future. It is gone. Finished. As is last night."

"Aye. Until they need her. She has promised to go to their aid if she can count on theirs."

"I would expect no less. But Jake, never mind the gang. Have you had no indication of her feelings?"

He shook his head. "She said something—but it was nothing."

Claire had to stop herself from smiling. Maggie rarely indulged in such. "What was this nothing?"

"She said, 'I want to go to university and raise my flock and live in my house with y—' But she didn't finish."

"You?" In Claire's mind, it could be nothing else. Which put a whole new complexion on Maggie's decision to trade her university career in Germany for a slightly less satisfying one in London.

To be closer to her flock? Or to Jake?

"I don't know, Lady. But that wee bit of a word has had me in tortures."

She took his arm again, and set off up the hill at a slow walk. "There is only one thing you can do. You must ask her straight out if she returns your affection."

After a moment, he said, "Do you mean to say you approve? I am no Lieutenant Terwilliger."

"She is no Lizzie," Claire pointed out. "But my two young men have promising careers in the Royal Aeronautic Corps, so there is no obstacle there. Far from it." Claire considered her next words carefully. "Maggie's grandfather wrote to me, so I know what passed between you. And while I cannot approve an engagement, Jake, until Maggie has finished her degree, neither he nor I have any objection to the two of you coming to an understanding."

He stopped in the cold grass as though unable to take another step. And when she looked up into his face, his eyes were swimming with tears. His mouth worked, the corners turning down in an effort at control, but no words came out.

So Claire answered the question that he could not ask. "Truly, dear. I have always known that you cherished a soft spot for Maggie, even as children. I have seen you grow into a man who is worthy of her—loyal—unafraid to put himself at risk for her sake … and most of all, who has shared both past hardships and past triumphs. Who *knows* her as no other man ever could. Jake, it seems as though you have been made for each other, though from the outside it seems no two people could be more different."

"Do—do you really think I could be worthy of her?" His voice wobbled, and two tears spilled over and made tracks down his cheeks. Reddening, he dashed them away.

Claire took both his hands in hers. "I think you are worthy of one another now."

At which point his self-possession failed him altogether, and he bent his head to rest it on her shoulder, his own shaking with sobs. Claire came near to tears herself, for these were not the sobs of sorrow, but a cataclysm of joy. Of hope. And of gratitude.

She hugged him, stretching up on tiptoe to pat his back, giving all the comfort she could until the storm passed. Then she pulled her handkerchief out of her sleeve and handed it to him.

"Tomorrow is Twelfth Night," she said, refusing the handkerchief when he tried to give it back afterward. "Maggie's first night in her new home. I have it from Davina that they are moored at Hatley House, so Lizzie and Tigg will be reunited and consequently out of the way. Alice and Ian, Dr. Malvern and I are invited there to dinner. I suggest that you find a reason to visit the cottage, and choose your moment with care."

Jake did not reply. Instead, he seized her gloved hand and kissed it.

And on the walk back up the hill, it seemed to Claire that his footsteps held the lightness of anticipation. Of hope.

In fact, she was almost tempted to check his boots, to see if they touched the ground at all.

CHAPTER 9

TWELFTH NIGHT 1896

*D*ue to the peculiar circumstances of her life, Maggie had not been in the habit of accumulating possessions. If an object could not be loaded on an airship at short notice, she had been in the habit of declining it. The furniture from Gwynn Place still surprised her every time she passed over her own threshold. So the move from Carrick House to Holly Cottage consisted of loading her trunk and two or three crates of books, linens, and perishables into the airfield's jalopy and chugging over the bridge to her new home.

Like a pair of excited grasshoppers, Alfred and Lucy dashed hither and yon with bedding and food and—in Alfred's case—pockets full of spare parts for the steam boiler and its connected stove and hot water system, which, along with the care of the hens and grounds, were to be his particular responsibility.

Jake built up the fire in the front parlor and lit it. Before long the cottage was snug and warm, and Maggie was able to preside over the brown teapot and the small spread of food, feeling as ridiculously proud as though she had been Lady Dunsmuir herself tonight, wearing her tawny diamond tiara at the foot of the great dining table at Hatley House.

As though Jake had divined her thoughts, he said, "Are you sorry not to be with them all?"

Maggie shook her head. "One, it was not a general invitation, and two, I said I wanted to be here to celebrate Twelfth Night, and here I am, with my own household about me."

Oh dear. She had made it sound as though she included Jake in her household. As though she expected him to be. Did he think she was being forward—presumptuous? She wracked her brain for something to say that might mitigate the damage, but for once, that trustworthy organ failed her.

"I brought a little something to go with Granny's fruitcake." Jake opened a bottle of French port, the kind Lewis imported for the club.

"I have no proper glasses." Thank goodness he had not seemed to notice her gaffe. "We will have to use our teacups."

On this singular occasion, and being Twelfth Night, Lucy and Alfred were both allowed a thimbleful of port with which to toast each other. Not long afterward, they washed the dishes and then took themselves off to bed, leaving Maggie and Jake before the fire in the wing chairs from Gwynn Place.

She gave a soft laugh. "We look like a pair of old folks, don't we?"

Oh dear, she had done it again! Would he think she had visions of a life together with him? That she wanted to grow old with him? Never mind if she did—if he did not share such feelings, then she may as well go upstairs herself and pull the quilts over her head to hide her humiliation.

"There is something to be said for surviving to a

respectable age." Jake's tone was conversational as he poured a little more port into her teacup. As though again, he had not noticed. Thank goodness for small mercies. "There have been times when I doubted we would make it this far."

"And now look at us." She toasted him, and wanted to smack herself. There was no *us*. Was it the port causing her tongue to flap like washing on a line? Or had the heat of the fire and the sense of its being the calm after the storm caused her usual reticence to relax to the point of reck-lessness?

"Now look at you," he said, watching her over the rim of his cup. "The queen of the south bank."

"Do not remind me. The events of last night have no place here."

"Forgive me, Maggie. I did not mean to spoil your first night in your own home."

"Nothing you could say would spoil it," she said softly. "I am just glad you are able to share it with me."

"You would rather have me than Lizzie?" he asked with a quizzical tilt to one eyebrow. In the firelight, his lean face was hollowed here and lit there, with a tawny cast that made him look like a pirate.

"I would not have taken her from Tigg this evening for all the world," she assured him. "Not that I could have. If she had been tied to a moving train, she still would have found a way."

"They are well matched, and she is happy," Jake said. Then, after a moment, he went on, "Mr. Alden Dean seems a gentle-manly sort."

Alden Dean? She had not given him a moment's thought from the minute he had practically fallen out of the landau on his friends' doorstep until now. "I suppose he is. He has a gentleman's education, and his friends are of the right sort, if one counts that kind of thing. If one is a Blood."

"But Wit or not, you will have that kind of education."

Now it was her turn to eye him. "What are you getting at, Jake?"

He shrugged, as if it didn't matter. "I just thought you would make a match of it, that's all. He seemed very interested."

She put down her empty teacup and stared at him outright. "After last night? You seriously think that he and I might do so after last night?"

"For a man who did not even know the south bank gangs existed before they smashed your windows, he acquitted himself fairly well," Jake said mildly. "He has a good touch with a cast-iron pan."

"I only hope he will keep the details to himself," she said, her gaze falling. "I never thought of it before—but think of the lengths the Lady must have gone to in order to keep her shadow life from becoming public. I do not much relish *that* should the word get out. I should likely be dismissed from the university."

"Let us not borrow trouble."

"You are a fine one to say so!"

He grinned at her. "At least you may be confident that I will not blab your secrets. Though it was tempting after the French invasion. To notify the newspapers or some such. You ought to have had a medal."

"Certainly not." She rose and cleared away the teacups. When she came out of the kitchen, Jake stood by the fire, gazing into it as though seeing pictures in the flames.

She joined him on the hearth. "It is getting late. I—I

suppose you will be wanting to return the jalopy to the airfield."

His quick gaze found hers. "Do you want me to go?"

"No, no. Not at all. I just…" She flushed. The fire was almost too warm, and she had exhausted her reserves of modesty. "Jake—"

"Maggie—" he said at the same time, then smiled. "Ladies first."

In that second of confusion, her resolve firmed. She must speak, though the cost was embarrassment and maybe even estrangement. She could not live another moment without knowing where she stood.

"I heard you say something last night, and I want to know what you meant by it," she said with a bald sort of desperation. "You called me *my dear little love.*"

He had gone still—the stillness of the watchman before the trumpet sounds. "You heard that?"

"I did."

"I thought you were unconscious."

Maggie frowned. "What did you mean? Why did you say such a thing?"

"Because … because I couldn't *not* say it. Not when you lay there in a pool of blood and I thought I had lost—" His throat worked. "That I was too late."

Somehow they had moved closer on the hearth, so that the firelight played over his face, and illuminated the green of his eyes.

"If I've offended you, Maggie, I am sorry."

"Offended me?" she said incredulously. "How could you? You, who stood at my side, risking your life?"

"Alden Dean did, too."

She made a rude noise and when he smiled, it only inflamed her more. "I never want to hear Alden Dean's name again. The things he said to me—such presumption. There is more to my life than men like that. And—and—blast and bebother it, Jake—*you* are part of that life."

His eyes widened, his dear eyes that had seen so much. Too much. Enough to give a man nightmares. And yet he had not hesitated to plunge into one more nightmare for her sake.

"I am," he said at last, his voice not much more than a whisper. "As a brother."

She gathered her courage to the sticking point. "I have many brothers. Claude. Lewis. Snouts. Tigg. I am not in need of brothers. I am in need of a man who chooses to stand beside me. Whom *I* choose. Here and now, and in the future."

"The man beside you here and now is not worthy of you," he croaked. "As much as he wants to be."

"And is the queen of the south bank gangs worthy of a navigator of Her Majesty's Aeronautic Corps?" she demanded. "Can you present me to your fleet commander without wondering how you are going to keep my obligations secret? Can you look Sir Ian in the eye and claim me the way he claims our Alice?"

He grasped her elbows. "Is that how you see yourself? As someone who must hide half herself from now on? Well, here is how I see you. The most beautiful woman I ever set eyes on. The bravest heroine who ever stood up to anyone—invasion—gangs—your awful grandmother. The kindest, most patient teacher and sister that any street sparrow ever had. Not one woman in a million could match you, Maggie Polgarth, save only the Lady and Alice—and it wasn't *their* grandfathers who gave me permission to court you. It was yours."

Maggie felt as though she had been stricken silent by her own lightning pistol. And truly, her veins were running with fire and ice at one and the same time. She was trembling with energy—and yet could not move a muscle.

"My grandfather?" she whispered.

"Aye."

"Said that? You asked him?"

"Well, not exactly." He seemed to realize he was holding her prisoner by her elbows, and relaxed his grip. "I asked him for the holly sapling, but what I got was his blessing. Your grandfather apparently has seen more than either of us—and he told the Lady so."

Up from the deepest, most hidden part of Maggie's character—up from the very ground, it seemed—came a wave of joy so great that she could hardly speak. "And what will you do with his permission, Jake McTavish?"

"I am not allowed to do anything with it." His hands slid down from her elbows, and her fingers twined with his as though they had been waiting years to do so. "The Lady says that I may not ask you to marry me until after you have your degree."

"Jake McTavish, have you been talking this over with everyone but me? I suppose you have asked Lizzie her permission, too?" But Maggie's voice trembled with laughter. It was all she could do to keep from shouting aloud and dancing about the room.

"I would not dare," he said with absolute truth, and this time she did laugh. And for the first time all evening, his face softened and his eyes took on an intensity that she had never seen in them before. "But if it meant having your love, I would take on Lizzie and anyone else who stood in my way. Do I have a chance, Maggie? Will you tell me I can hope?"

She did not know how she could contain such joy. So she threw her arms around him—so forward—goodness, what would the Lady say? But she was not here. Jake's arms went around her so tightly she could barely breathe, but she relished it.

"You have more than a chance," she whispered into the dear hollow she had just discovered under his ear. "You have more than hope. You have my heart. You always have had it. And you always will."

After that, no more needed to be said. They stood there in the firelight, holding each other close, and for the first time, she fell into a man's kiss. A man who had been saving that gift only for her. It was as though Maggie had been sailing in rough seas all her life, and she had finally found her way to a safe harbor.

Neither of them saw the two little figures in nightdresses sitting silently at the top of the stairs. Lucy grasped Alfred's hand and held it tight. He raised their joined hands over his head in a victory salute. And both of them clapped their other hands over their mouths, rocking in breathless joy at the happiness filling Holly Cottage on its very first night as their home.

THE END

AFTERWORD

Dear reader,

I hope you enjoyed reading the adventures of Maggie, Jake, Lady Claire and the gang in the Magnificent Devices world as much as I enjoy writing them. It is your support and enthusiasm that is like the steam in an airship's boiler, keeping the entire enterprise afloat and ready for the next adventure.

You might leave a review on your favorite retailer's site to tell others about the books. And you can find print, digital, and audiobook editions of the series online. I hope to see you over at my website, www.shelleyadina.com, where you can sign up for my newsletter and be the first to know of new releases and special promotions. You'll also receive a free short story set in the Magnificent Devices world just for subscribing!

Interested in reading more? You might join the adventures of Daisy and Frederica Linden, two young ladies from Bath, in the Mysterious Devices series.

Following is an excerpt. Fair winds!

Shelley

EXCERPT

THE BRIDE WORE CONSTANT WHITE
COPYRIGHT 2018 BY SHELLEY ADINA

Chapter 1

July 1895
Bath, England

It is a truth universally acknowledged that a young woman of average looks, some talent, and no fortune must be in want of a husband, the latter to be foisted upon her at the earliest opportunity lest she become an embarrassment to her family. This had been depressingly borne in upon Miss Margrethe Amelia Linden, known to her family and her limited number of intimate friends as Daisy, well before the occasion of her twenty-first birthday.

"Certainly you cannot go to a ball, escorted or not," said her Aunt Jane. "You are not out of mourning for your dear mother. It would not be suitable. I am surprised that you have even brought it up, Daisy."

Daisy took a breath in order to defend herself, but her aunt forestalled her with a raised salad fork.

"No, I will invite a very few to lunch—including one or two suitable young men. Now that you have come into my sister's little bit of money, you will be slightly more attractive to a discerning person than, perhaps, you might have been before. Mr. Fetherstonehaugh, now. He still cherishes hopes of you, despite your appalling treatment of him. I insist on your considering him seriously. His father owns a manufactory of steambuses in Yorkshire, and he is the only boy in a family of five."

"I do not wish to be attractive to any of the gentlemen of our acquaintance, Aunt." *Particularly not to him.* "They lack gumption. To say nothing of chins."

This had earned her an expression meant to be crushing, but which only succeeded in making Aunt Jane look as though her lunch had not agreed with her.

"Your uncle and I wish to see you safely settled, dear," she said with admirable restraint.

Aunt Jane prided herself on her restraint under provocation. She had become rather more proud of it in the nearly two years since her sister had brought her two daughters to live under her roof, and then passed on to her heavenly reward herself. When one's sister's husband was known to have gone missing in foreign parts, one was also subject to impertinent remarks. Therefore, her restraint had reached heroic proportions.

"When you have been married fifty years, like our beloved Queen, you will know that a chin or lack thereof is hardly a consideration in a good husband—while a successful manufactory certainly is."

Daisy was not sure if Aunt Jane had meant to insult the prince, who from all accounts was still quite an attractive man. It was true that she could no more imagine Her Majesty without her beloved Albert than the sun without a moon. They had a scandalous number of children—nine!—and still the newspapers had reported that they had danced until dawn at Lord and Lady Dunsmuir's ball in London earlier in the week. Her Majesty was said to be prodigiously fond of dancing—between that and childbirth, she must be quite the athlete.

Daisy had never danced until dawn in her life, and doing so seemed as unlikely as having children.

Especially now.

For as of ten days ago, she was no longer a genteel spinster of Margaret's Buildings, Bath, but a woman of twenty-one years and independent means, having procured not only a letter of credit from her bank, but a ticket from Bath to London, and subsequently, passage aboard the packet to Paris, where she had boarded the transatlantic airship *Persephone* bound for New York.

"My goodness, you're so brave," breathed Emma Makepeace, her breakfast companion in the grand airship's dining saloon this morning, the third of their crossing. She had been listening with rapt attention, her spoonful of coddled egg halting in its fatal journey. "But at what point did you realize you were not alone?"

Daisy glanced at her younger sister, Frederica, who wisely did not lift her own attention from her plate, but continued to shovel in poached eggs, potatoes, and sliced ham glazed in orange sauce as though this were her last meal.

"As we were sailing over the Channel. At that point, my sister deemed it safe to reveal herself, since there would be no danger of my sending her back to our aunt and uncle." She gave a sigh. "We are committed to this adventure together, I am afraid."

"I certainly am," Freddie ventured. "I used all my savings for the tickets, including what I could beg from Maggie Polgarth."

"Who is that?" Miss Makepeace asked, resuming her own breakfast with a delicate appetite. "One of your school friends?"

Freddie nodded. "Maggie and her cousin Elizabeth Seacombe are the wards of Lady Claire Malvern, of Carrick House in Belgravia."

"Oh, I have met Lady Claire. Isn't she lovely? What an unexpected pleasure it is to meet people acquainted with her."

While Daisy recovered from her own surprise at a reliable third party knowing people she had half believed to be imaginary, Freddie went on.

"With Lady Claire's encouragement, both Maggie and Lizzie own shares in the railroads *and* the Zeppelin Airship Works, though they are only eighteen—my own age. But that is beside the point." Another glance at Daisy, who had been caught by the deep golden color of the marmalade in her spoon.

If she were to paint a still life at this very moment, she would use lemon yellow, with a bit of burnt umber, and some scarlet lake—just a little—for the bits of orange peel embedded deep within.

"The point?" Miss Makepeace inquired, and Daisy came back to herself under their joint regard. It was up to her to redirect the course of the conversation.

"The point is that, having had some number of astonishing adventures—I have my doubts about the veracity of some of them—Miss Polgarth was all too forthcoming in her encouragement of my sister's desertion of her responsibilities to school and family."

"You deserted yours, too," Freddie pointed out. "Poor Mr. Fetherstonehaugh. He is not likely to recover his heart very soon."

"Oh dear." Miss Makepeace was one of those fortunate individuals who would never have to settle for the chinless and suitable of this world. For she was a young woman of considerable looks and some means, despite the absence of anyone resembling a chaperone or a lady's maid. Perhaps that individual kept herself to her cabin. Her clothes were not showy, but so beautiful they made Daisy ache inside—the pleats perfection, the colors becoming, the lace handmade. Clearly her time in Paris before boarding *Persephone* had been well spent in purchasing these delights.

Miss Makepeace had been blessed with hair the shade of melted caramel and what people called an "English skin." Daisy, being as English as anyone, had one too by default, but hers didn't have the perfect shades of a rose petal. Nor did her own blue eyes possess that deep tint verging on violet. At least Daisy's hair could be depended on—reddish-brown in some lights and with enough wave in it to make it easy to put up— unlike poor Freddie, who had inherited Mama's lawless dark curls. No one would be clamoring at the door to paint Daisy, but Miss Makepeace—oh, she was a horse of a different color.

She absolutely must persuade her to sit for a portrait in watercolors.

But talk of poor Mr. Fetherstonehaugh had brought the ghost of a smile to their companion's face, so Daisy thought it prudent not to abandon the subject of gentlemen just yet, despite its uncomfortable nature. They had been in the air for three days, and after the second day, had found one another convivial enough company that they had begun looking for each other at meals, and spending the afternoons together embroidering or (in Daisy's case) sketching. The lavish interiors of *Persephone* fairly begged to be painted in her travel journal. In all that time Daisy had not seen Miss Makepeace smile. Not a real one. But now, one had nearly trembled into life, and she would use Mr. Fetherstonehaugh ruthlessly if it meant coaxing it into full bloom.

"Have you ever been to Bath, Miss Makepeace?" she asked, spreading marmalade on the toast.

"Only once, when I was a girl," she said. "Papa's business keeps him in London and New York nearly exclusively, and after Mama passed away, I did not have a companion with whom to go to such places. I remember it being very beautiful," she said wistfully. "And at the bottom of the Royal Crescent is a gravel walk. I wondered if it could be the very one where Captain Wentworth and Anne Elliot walked after all was made plain between them."

Frederica, being of a literal turn of mind, blinked at her. "They were not real, Miss Makepeace."

The English skin colored a little. "I know. But it was a pretty fancy, for the time it took me to walk down the hill to the gate."

"Poor Mr. Fetherstonehaugh," Daisy said on a sigh. "He attempted to quote Jane Austen to me while we were dancing in the parlor of one of my aunt's acquaintance three weeks ago."

"That sounds most promising in a man," Miss Makepeace said.

"But it was the first sentences of *Pride and Prejudice*, Miss Makepeace." She leaned in. "And they were said in reference *to himself*."

To her delight, the smile she had been angling for blossomed into life. "Dear me. Miss Austen would be appalled."

"My sentiments exactly. And when he turned up on my aunt's doorstep the next morning proposing himself as the companion of my future life, I took my example from Elizabeth Bennet on the occasion of *her* first proposal. I fear the allusion was lost on him, however." She frowned. "He called me a heartless flirt."

Miss Makepeace covered her mouth with her napkin and Daisy could swear it was to muffle a giggle. "You are no such thing," she said when she could speak again. "I should say it was a near escape."

"Our aunt would not agree," Freddie put in. "She and my uncle have very strong feelings about indigent relations and their burden upon the pocketbook."

"Granted, it is not their fault their pocketbook is slender," Daisy conceded. "But that is no reason to push us on every gentleman who stops to smell the roses nodding over the wall."

"How do you come to be aboard *Persephone*?" Freddie asked their companion shyly.

She was not yet out, so had not had many opportunities to go about in company. Add to this a nearly paralyzing shyness —for reasons both sisters kept secret, and despite the misleading behavior of her hair—and it still astonished Daisy that she had had the gumption to follow her all the way to London with nothing but her second-best hat and a valise containing three changes of clothes, her diary, and a canvas driving coat against bad weather.

Now it was Miss Makepeace who leaned in, the lace covering her fine bosom barely missing the marmalade on her own toast. "Can you keep a secret?"

"Oh, yes," Freddie said eagerly.

Which was quite true. Among other things, she had concealed from everyone—except perhaps that deplorable Maggie Polgarth—her plans to run away and accompany Daisy on her mission.

"I am what is known as a mail-order bride." Miss Makepeace sat back to enjoy the effect of this confidence on her companions.

"A what?" Freddie said after a moment, when no clarification seemed to be forthcoming.

"There is no such thing," Daisy said a little flatly. Well, it was better than sitting and gaping like a flounder.

"There I must contradict you." Miss Makepeace aligned her knife and fork in the middle of her plate, and the waiter, seeing this signal, whisked it away. "In the guise of a literary club, I have been meeting these last six months in London with a group of young ladies determined to make their own fortunes. An agency assisted us in finding the best matches of ability and temperament in places as far-flung as the Canadas and the Louisiana Territory."

"There are agencies for this sort of thing?" Daisy managed under the shock of this fresh information. It was lucky that Aunt Jane was as ignorant of these facts as Daisy herself had been until this moment, or heaven knew where Daisy might have been shipped off to by now.

And what was a young woman like Miss Makepeace, with

every blessing of breeding and beauty, doing applying as a mail-order bride? It defied understanding.

Miss Makepeace nodded. "I have been writing to Mr. Bjorn Hansen, of Georgetown, for some months, and am convinced that he will make me a good husband." She touched the exceedingly modest diamond upon the fourth finger of her left hand. "He sent this in his last letter, and I sent my acceptance by return airship."

"My goodness," Freddie breathed. "I have never met a mail-order bride. I thought they only existed in the flickers—you know, like *Posted to Paradise*." She and Daisy had stood in the queue outside the nickelodeon on Milsom Street for half an hour to see that one, much to their aunt's disgust. But it had been so romantic!

"We are quite real, I assure you." Two dimples dented Miss Makepeace's cheeks. "My suit and veil are in my trunk. I will meet Mr. Hansen in person for the first time when I alight in Georgetown, and we will be married two days later in the First Presbyterian Church on Taos Street. It is all arranged."

"Where is Georgetown, exactly?" Daisy asked.

Not that it mattered—she and Frederica were bound for Santa Fe, on a quest that could not be postponed. Their father, Dr. Rudolph Linden, had been missing for nearly two years. Influenza had taken their mother last winter—hastened, Daisy was certain, by the anxiety and depression she had suffered after his mysterious disappearance. Now that she had reached her majority, Daisy was determined to take up the search where her mother had left off. And this time, if love and determination meant anything, she and Freddie would find him.

"It is in the northern reaches of the Texican Territories, in the mountains," Miss Makepeace explained in answer to her question. "From Denver, it is merely an hour west by train. It is said to be one of the loveliest towns in the territory—and certainly one of the richest. Silver, you know. It is surrounded by mines on every side, and has a bustling economy, I am told."

A young man who had been passing on the way to his table now hesitated next to theirs. "I do beg your pardon. Forgive me for intruding, but are you speaking of Georgetown?"

If Aunt Jane had been sitting opposite, Daisy had no doubt there would have been either the cut direct—or an invitation to breakfast if she thought the young man might be good husband material. But they were en route for a continent where one might stop and strike up a conversation without having to be formally introduced by a mutual acquaintance—or to give one's family antecedents back four generations.

"We are, sir. Do you know it?"

His square, honest face broke into a smile, and Daisy noted with interest the quality of the velvet lapels on his coat, and the fashionable leaf-brown color of his trousers—not the dull brown of earth, but the warmer tones of the forest in autumn.

"I am bound there as well. Please allow me to introduce myself. My name is Hugh Meriwether-Astor, originally from Philadelphia. I have recently bought a share in the Pelican mine."

"And are you going out to inspect your investment, or have you been there before?" Miss Makepeace asked.

"This is my first visit. I'm afraid I have an ulterior motive —that of escaping the bad temper of my older brother, who is not quite so conservative in his business dealings. I should like to get my hands dirty, and do a little excavating myself if I can, before I go back to law school. And you?"

As the eldest, and practically a married woman, Miss Makepeace made the introductions. Daisy noted that she did not vouchsafe any personal details of their voyage, she supposed because she had no personal observations of her future home to offer him. They parted with promises of seeing one another at the card tables after dinner, and the young man continued to his table by the viewing port.

"What a nice person," Frederica ventured. "He does not seem much older than you, Daisy, and yet he owns part of a mine. His family must be rather well off."

"If my facts are in order, he is closely connected to the Meriwether-Astor Manufacturing Works in Philadelphia," Miss Makepeace said in a low tone. Heaven forbid the young man should know they were discussing him. "Surely even in Bath you will have read in the papers about his cousin, Gloria Meriwether-Astor, who owns the company."

"It's a difficult name to miss," Daisy said. "Wasn't she the one who singlehandedly stopped a war in the Wild West and returned home in triumph with none other than a railroad baron's long-lost heir for a husband?"

Honestly, while it might have been quite true, it did sound like one of the sensational plots beloved of the flickers.

"I am sure it wasn't singlehandedly," Miss Makepeace said. "But I will say that the union of two such industrial fortunes made headlines in the Fifteen Colonies, and London and Zurich as well. It was all any of my father's cronies talked of at dinner for weeks."

"My friend Maggie knows her," Freddie said most unexpectedly. "Gloria, I mean. Mrs. Stanford Fremont."

"Nonsense," Daisy said. Honestly, she was becoming very tired of these references. "Another of that girl's absurd fabrications."

"It isn't!" Freddie drew back, affronted, and refused to speak for the rest of their meal.

There were some misfortunes for which one could only be thankful.

I hope you'll continue the adventure by purchasing The Bride Wore Constant White. Thank you!

Shelley

ALSO BY SHELLEY ADINA

STEAMPUNK

The Magnificent Devices series

Lady of Devices

Her Own Devices

Magnificent Devices

Brilliant Devices

A Lady of Resources

A Lady of Spirit

A Lady of Integrity

A Gentleman of Means

Devices Brightly Shining (Christmas novella)

Fields of Air

Fields of Iron

Fields of Gold

Carrick House (novella)

Selwyn Place (novella)

Holly Cottage (novella)

Gwynn Place (novella)

The Mysterious Devices series

The Bride Wore Constant White

The Dancer Wore Opera Rose

The Matchmaker Wore Mars Yellow

The Engineer Wore Venetian Red

The Judge Wore Lamp Black

The Professor Wore Prussian Blue

ABOUT THE AUTHOR

Shelley Adina is the author of 24 novels published by Harlequin, Warner, and Hachette, and more than a dozen more published by Moonshell Books, Inc., her own independent press. She writes steampunk and contemporary romance as Shelley Adina; as Adina Senft, writes Amish women's fiction; and as Charlotte Henry, writes classic Regency romance. She holds an MFA in Writing Popular Fiction, and is currently working on her PhD in Creative Writing at Lancaster University in the UK. She won RWA's RITA Award® in 2005, and was a finalist in 2006. When she's not writing, Shelley is usually quilting, sewing historical costumes, or enjoying the garden with her flock of rescued chickens.

Shelley loves to talk with readers about books, chickens, and costuming!
www.shelleyadina.com
www.charlotte-henry.com
shelley@shelleyadina.com